I0683790

CAVE

the story of a girl

Laura Ross

Staten House

Staten House

Follow me around: **IG**: *lmwrites50*

contents

Prologue

"You know what I can make you do." Rachel whispered menacingly in my ear.

Behind her stood the crowd of my former best friend crew who I, at one point, couldn't imagine life without. Now they just looked at me. Sneering. Cackling at the current fat girl who used to be their skinny best friend. I think about my *tia* Adriana, my mother's twin sister who'd always been on the chubbier side, who had to fight her way through public school during situations like these.

"You got to show them you ain't nothing to fuck with!" She jeered during a visit after I told her about my bullies back home. "Roll them sleeves up, don't cave."

Don't cave, I think as I study the group of white girls encircling me and backing me into the lockers. I loved

1

my *tia*, but some of her methods were a bit questionable. Fear iced my veins as I stared at them, all so tall and hovering over my shorter frame like a murder of crows waiting for a bite. Then Rachel shoves me again, so hard this time though my vision blurs and glasses fall to the linoleum floor.

"Bitch are you even listening to me?!"

I didn't say anything. Just squinted at the blurry group of teens laughing at me getting my ass beat. Rachel Frasier, the mousey girl I befriended in second grade, was now throwing me against lockers. Slapping my food tray onto the floor during lunch and sometimes following me into the restroom. Tears misted in my eyes at the humiliation I felt when she'd make me go pee in front of an entire crowd of jocks who'd sneak in after I entered.

"Female Anatomy 101." She laughed, her foot propping my stall door open for all the guys to see. "Or shall I say, Selfish whore Anatomy 101?"

"I'm sorry!" I wailed then and now while Rachel's ice blue eyes pierced mine. "I don't know how else to make it up to you. What do you want from me?"

"The Randon's are responsible for his death. You and that shitty attorney dad of yours perpetuate lies to keep yourselves protected. How many times do I have to say it before you get it, Simone?"

I sink to the floors of the empty halls. School had let out twenty minutes ago, but everyone knew not to mess with Rachel Frasier. Her dad, or Principal Frasier we called him, let her have free reign to do in these halls what she wanted.

Like torture girls like me for killing her uncle.

"I didn't do it!" I cried.

A swift kick to my gut made me howl in pain as I writhed on the ground. I didn't know who did it, but the point was made.

"It's time you pay for what your family's done to mine. *Bestie*." She spat sarcastically as she knelt beside me.

From my vantage point, the knife was visible in her perfectly polished hand.

"It wasn't me! You gotta believe me!" I begged, my voice coarse from the beating and kick to the gut.

I didn't let my mind wander down there, towards memory lane, since the craziness from that entire court case destroyed my life. And ruined so many others in the making. She's right though. Things never would have gotten this bad if it wasn't for my dad's actions and mother's convenient ignorance. It left me to deal with the reality of what happened. What was that reality?

Blood on our hands. My entire family's.

"You think those were my uncle's last words before he was shot to death?" Rachel asked, sliding the blade gently across my neck and upper chest.

"I don't know." I cried again.

"Well you're about to know, aren't you?" She laughed, triggering the rest of the crew above us to cackle like the hivemind they were. Like I used to be.

"Stab that bitch, Rache!" The voice of Katina Hirsham cheered within the crowd. Another one of my former best friends who'd rightfully abandoned me after the court case ended.

I lost everything. My friends, some of my family, and gained so much weight in the aftermath of that case's conclusion that I barely left my house anymore. Nobody could pull me out to the light. And I preferred to stay buried inside until there was nobody left to hurt me. No feelings, either.

I cringed as the sting of the blade entered my flesh. Not deep enough to do much harm, but enough to wake me up. A surge of adrenaline, or maybe insanity, sent me sitting up and grabbing the knife from her bony hands.

"Fight back *mija*. Don't let them win. Don't cave!" *Tia's* words came to me as soon as the screams did. I barely realized what I just done or the charges surely to come after I leapt to my feet and ran towards the doors.

"That crazy bitch stabbed Rachel!" One of them screamed behind me as I sprinted to the parking lot where my car was singularly parked. "Get her!"

Breathing heavy, I closed my eyes tight to avoid the blood on my hands from what I'd just done. It wasn't right, but I clung to the frayed principles ingrained in me by my *tia* to get me through the next few minutes.

After all, I couldn't let them see me CAVE.

Chapter One

TUNING IN TO MADNESS

I guess I was always the fat ass. You know, the butt of the joke? It wasn't like I was always this way. I wasn't just "born fat." It was a long time ago when I picked up that carb-infested doughnut and fruit punch drink and decided to end it all: My friendships with the skinny, the life of my formal socially accepted figure, and my shallowness. And it wasn't the fact that I cracked under pressure; I pretty much just said "stop." I didn't want that sort of life any longer, and there wasn't a way I would've kept it going. So, I put my low self esteem aside and did that for myself.

"Simone! They've arrived!" My overly-cheerful-mother, Ashleigh Randon, sang.

With her, my equally merry father Zachary Randon, carrying the stash. Granted, I was eating and watching television in our red room. Yes, this was my family. Weird.

The red room was the television room, the purple was the reading room, the yellow was the dining room and the blue room was the "cooking quarters" as my mother called it. It was seriously a freaky kitchen, but she was old and set in that cheery mindset. Mom was like the weather: you could predict what she would do, but you'd never change her. She was also the receptionist for the eye doctors my glasses came from, unfortunately, which was called "The Family Eye."

My mother was a gorgeous, statuesque, latina who posed as the complete opposite of her twin sister, Adrianna. Where my aunt was more stern and professional, my mother was a recovering hippie. "Glasses for my Simone Princessa de Randon!" She chirped while handing them to me. Sadly, that was my real name.

"Mom! Thank you! I'm busy... please leave!" I took the glasses from her and shoved them into my pocket.

My father, a proud African American man and Public Defender, looked and seemed chagrined when he came forward and said, "Simone, calm yourself. Your mother is merely being your mother, now just take the glasses and we'll be on our way."

I sighed; he was always being the problem solver, party pooper. He worked for the public defense team to combat the many crimes in Burlington, New Jersey. So it was basically his *job* to be a problem solver.

I did as he asked and escorted them to the door. On their faces was evident disappointment and surprise. I knew what they were thinking, moodier than usual.

Escaping the colored room, I grabbed my cell and texted:

ME: Where r u? To my best friend Seth Montgomery.

His answer was instant:

SETH: U kno where I am, Sim. The sk8 park.

Seth Montgomery befriended me in my third year in elementary school—we were seniors now. Seth was actually an Eminem look-a-like in his features. Well, they had the same dangerous air to them. They didn't look much alike in truth; just reminded me of each other. Besides, Seth hated it when I called him Eminem, which was all the more reason I still called him that. Despite that, Seth was currently one of the tallest of our senior class. With me standing at a miniature five-two at his side, it was nearly impossible for me to hug his six-foot-six frame. He was actually sort of gangly in freshman year and had horrible acne. But hey, the underdogs had to stick together, right? I cleared my throat, grabbed my sweater, and started for the skate park. Even though it was a warm August afternoon and I was already wearing dark jeans and a gray t-shirt, I didn't want anyone to see my, "excess body weight". Really though, I was sort of self conscious of my body, and Seth hated that. Whenever I would hide when I saw people or cover up, he'd get frustrated. I mean, it was my body, right?

Shaking my head, I began to walk the short distance to Riot, the skating park Seth frequented. On the way though, I happened to pass a lot of weird stares. It was as if I could read their faces instead of them actually saying anything. *Girl, are you high? Is that some sort of family tradition? Do you know what time of year this is? Are you high?*

I rolled my eyes and made my way through the gates that led to Riot. Looking around, I noticed the lot of New Jersey's Puerto Ricans gawking at me as if I carried a nuclear bomb. I kept my gaze low and continued onward.

"Hey man—is she on something?" One of the dudes asked incredulously.

The other guy laughed and said, "I don't know, Tone. Let's ask her. Hey Sim!"

I recognized Seth's voice anywhere. Sighing deeply, I turned and glared at the tall jerk from a few feet away. Grinding my teeth, I stomped toward him and said, "I came to you for solace." He shared a look with the Puerto Rican guy, who I assumed to be 'Tone.'

"Yeah, sure. *Anything* for you babe!" He exaggerated.

I punched him on the arm. "Oh, shut up and come support me." He shrugged with a bright smile and allowed me to lead him to a place of privacy so we could talk. The place was just behind a skate ramp that neared the outer gates of the park. No one really ever skated here and I was all too thankful for that now.

"What is it, Sim?" He asked— his tone humorous. After I hesitated and began averting my gaze in several other directions he frowned and asked, "Sim?" laden with worry.

Seth's hands were on my shoulders now and when I peered up into his eyes a wave of dread washed over me. I had forgotten how psychiatrist-like my best friend could be. I reached into my pocket, uncased and put my glasses on my face.

"What do you think?" I asked dryly.

Seth folded his arms across his toned chest and studied me, "I think you're beautiful, Simone." His gaze was mentally undressing certain areas of my body I didn't think appropriate to describe.

I folded my arms over my chest and frowned at him. Jeez, his staring made me feel so exposed. "I meant the *glasses* Eminem."

Seth put his arms to his sides then and said smiling, "My name is Seth Montgomery thank you very much."

He said the words petulantly actually. Now that made me grin and decide to continue on with it.

"Then will the real Slim Shady please stand up?" At the mention of one of his favorite songs, Seth began to do a little dance, which looked very awkward considering how tall he was. I was nearly keeling over in laughter when I said, "You are *such* a white boy!"

Chapter Two

Glaring Daggers and Smiling Hand Grenades

"This is so stupid!" I exclaimed, laughing my ass off.

I was in my room watching the stupidest thing: a Barbie commercial about a fairy princess. It was like, Barbie was heading off to her third period class when—poof!—she's a magical princess. I don't know it just seemed crazy to me. What wasn't so princess was my reality.

Monday morning rolled around and I knew where I was supposed to be: Wal-Mart. Yes, unfortunately, I had to take on a summer job because my parents agreed that I was, "at that age." Jeez, parents were so damn annoying and grown-up. Rolling my eyes at the thought, I took my keys from my dresser and headed to the garage.

On the drive, I turned on the radio and began to sing along to the familiar song, "Meet Me Halfway," by the Black Eyed Peas. The song actually made me think of a few things for some reason. It made me think of school and how much I would miss it when I graduated. I had no idea why, but I always loved school. My friends—a.k.a. Seth—always teased me for being so different. Maybe I *was* different for liking school, heck, maybe I was for having a song like this make me *recollect* on school. Shrugging at no one in particular, I made a right and pulled into the spacious parking lot and parked. I was actually feeling kind of groovy until I walked in to a sight I *really* didn't want to see.

"HEY MOMO!" Georgia Cooper, the new fifteen-year old employee and my new trainee, greeted.

She was black and of average height and slim stature with the shiniest braces I'd ever seen. Surprisingly though, she rocked it. She was the kid in town from New York and had the weird accent and strange analogies long micro braids. I had to give the girl credit; she was smart. Georgia was the youngest employee at Wal-Mart, and this was sort of against the law, but she was an asset this place couldn't pass over. She worked the register with so much ease and swiftness I worried for my job for a time. I mean, her family had only been here two weeks and was already drawing more enemies than a fly to hard candy. Rolling my eyes at the analogy, I trudged inside and gave the kid a weary look.

"Hello Georgia."

She bent down to give me a hug, oh yeah she was taller than me and I'm eighteen, which was a shame. "Guess what, girl?"

I sighed; she was going to tell me anyway. "What?"

She bounced in excitement and squealed, "School's in, like, four days!" She did a little dance that made her look ultra skinny. "I'm gonna be in high school! Eureka!"

"Oh joy." I said dryly.

The last thing I wanted was a freshman to babysit on my first day back. I scoffed, that would totally make my senior year suck. I sauntered over to where my register was and readied myself for the oncoming shit storm of customers.

"Hey Momo, can I ask just one more question?"

"No." I answered tartly.

She sighed and began to bounce up and down all crazy like. "Well, if you don't let me ask I'm gonna keep bouncing until it annoys you. Momo!"

"WHAT!" I could feel my face heat up, and it was how I knew I should walk away from this child. I did just that and to my surprise, she followed me. I took deep breaths for strength and decided to do this anyway. "What is it, dearest Georgia?"

Rolling her eyes, she said, "Finally! Well, as I was saying, my...um..." She seemed embarrassed now.

Too bad I was in no mood for sympathy. "Spit it out Georgia." I said through clenched teeth.

She was looking down now and fiddling with her feet. "I was wondering, since you're one of my closest friends, if you can take me to school on the first day. I mean, I don't really know anyone here and...oh, never mind." I could tell that she was battling with herself, and I instantly felt for her. I sighed; she should really just come out and ask me like a human being once in a while.

"Of course, I'll give you a ride, Georgia. Just tell me where you live and I'll swing by around seven thirty. Kay?"

Georgia's face lit up warmly and gave me one of the tightest hugs I'd ever received in my life. "I so love you Simone." She squealed and added with a curious face, "Oh, and neat glasses by the way. Can I try them on?" I sighed sharply, took my glasses from hell off and handed them to her. Jeez, whatever it took to silence her was good enough for me. "Yeah, yeah, yeah—now go stack those paper towels and I'll see you in a bit."

Hours later, I found myself driving home in the night and on a quiet road and listening to a plethora of Black Eyed Peas songs. *"I've had the time of my life, and I owe it all to you!"* I had been screaming the lyrics when a realization struck me: School was in four days. At the thought of that I began to frown. Damn, that totally killed my buzz. I was gnawing on my lip nervously at the thought of facing my former enemies again—like Rachel Frazier. Yes, as cliché as it sounded, Rachel was the bully of the school and one of my worst nightmares. The skinny blonde used to be my BFF in middle school, but due to my excess bodyweight accumulation over the years she'd grown to fully hate me. I could actually remember the first wrong she did by me, and it was in eighth grade. I'd had the *biggest* crush on Wilson Jakes and I told Rachel and she basically stabbed me in the back by telling him in front of everyone. They all laughed and later on I ran into her on her knees before Wilson and doing very unnatural things with her mouth to him...

Anyway, it was gruesome, and we were no longer friends. End of story. Even though it was the end didn't mean the scars she inflicted were healed. She hated me and I was very weary of her. It was a strange relationship really, but who could blame her? After all, nobody wants to hang around the weird interracial girl, right?

People punished me because my father was black and white and my mother was strictly Puerto Rican. My mother always told me that people who didn't like who I was were haters, and that they were only jealous because I had the best of three worlds. I always saw it as people hating my light brown skin and dark brown curls that I was born with. Well, it was fair to say I just about hated myself.

I reached out to surf the Black Eyed Peas CD and found the one I wanted. I had been humming "Rock Your Body" when a car skidded in front of me. I slammed on brakes too late and crashed head-on into the back of the white sedan that made me think of the irony of the song I was jamming to in my head.

Chapter Three

An Internet Disputation

"Oh my fucking gosh! Are you okay?" I could hear the panicked voice from a distance. I felt as if I was fading in and out of consciousness and lying on a cloud. The cloud was soft and held me ever so lovingly. Funny, I felt a light drizzle on my arm and wondered if I should go inside or not. Should I? I saw a bright light and thought of one of those cheap sayings "don't walk into the light!" Huh, how very odd that that didn't sound like such a bad idea. Maybe what I needed was to step into the light and finally go home, inside. Sighing, I took a step forward but was halted by the manic voice.

"OH MY GOD! I FREAKING KILLED HER! OH MY...!"

No, *you didn't. I'm fine.* I assured. What was this person freaking out about anyway? "Will *you please wake up?*"

The deep lulling voice was entreating me and I felt like crap because I couldn't help him out. "*Dude, I am awake! Can't you hear me?*" And then there was more rain, it was falling harder this time, and I began to frantically wipe it off of me. Ugh! I thought it would be wise to go inside, away from the rain. So I was currently at a standstill, confused. Should I go inside, or stay out in the rain? I began my journey home, when I felt the worst pain of my life throughout my entire body. My head, legs, arms, shoulders, back, stomach...everywhere! I gasped as I opened my eyes to take in my surroundings. "*Unh!*" I groaned in agony when a figure, silhouetted by the night, sped toward me. "Oh, my God! Are you all right?" His voice was urgent, but not as frenzied as before. It hurt to open my eyes and speak, but I was able to sit upright. My former position had been my head resting against my steering wheel and my hands dangling limply at my sides. My throat was so dry that I was shocked when I managed to choke out, "What happened?"

"Thank God!" He exclaimed in a prominent Yankee accent. The stranger began to wave his hands in the air reassuringly as he crouched beside my side in the car. "It's okay. I called the ambulance, they should be here. And my insurance can cover this—it's okay now." He was rubbing my shoulder now, and that action made it hurt all the more. "Ah!" I groaned.

"Sorry! U-Um, I can wait on the curb over there for the ambulance to arrive if you want. Um—" I held my hand up in dismissal, which hurt like hell. I shook my head choking out, "Just tell me where I am." He nodded quickly and popped his head up to study the environment. "I'm not that sure. I just moved here not too long ago, and I don't really know my way around." He squinted into the night. "But I think this is the exit heading out of highway ninety five." His light brown eyes found mine and I noticed that he had braids hanging from his head that were just as long as my hair was—very long. He was tanned skinned and pretty toned from what I could tell from the muscles bulging from his thin white t-shirt. He was also wearing black sweats and slides with thick socks on; he looked as if he just came from track practice or something. When his eyes found mine, they were filled with so much concern I thought I'd crumble under the intensity of it. I could tell he'd been crying from before and that's when I looked down to catch a tear damp my arm. Looking up, I said, "I thought I was dead." The last thing I heard before the blaring noise of the ambulance was him whispering very softly, "I'm so sorry."

***

"¡Dios mio!" Came my mother's voice from the other end of my door. Sighing, I sat up in the hospital bed and awaited my frantic duo of parents. Sure enough, my mother exploded into the room and nearly fainted when she saw that I was okay. "Oh, you're just a little bruised, thank God!" My father walked in behind her and frowned at me before saying. "I'm going to kill the little bastard who did this to you." He pulled his cell phone out. "By God, I'll have every lawyer in town on his ass." I turned to my mother frantically. "Mom, I'm okay. I swear. You guys don't have to do this—"

"Shh, baby," Her hand was there, caressing my face. "You're father's an attorney—what did you expect?" My face was more panicked when she rolled her eyes. "Oh, sweetie, we're only doing this for your protection. We love you baby." She studied me from head to toe then. "Baby, did you eat? You look a little thin."

I snorted at that. "Thin? Me?" I reached my hand out to place it over her forehead. "Are *you* okay in there? The day I'm thin is the day I'll smile and actually mean it." My mom removed my hand and her features softened a degree. "I can't wait till the day you begin to accept yourself—how beautiful you are—"

"Mom, I don't want to have this argument with you right now. I'm fat, that's that. It's over." She averted her eyes and said distantly. "That boy has been waiting out there for you for a while now. He says his name is Jerome or something." I nodded, and that's when my father approached us. His expression was stoic when he said, "I have my people on it, and it's taken care of now." He sighed before he said, "Are you okay sweetheart?" I nodded and said quickly. "It's only a little soreness and some swelling. The doctor said he found no concussion and that I can go home tonight." I swallowed. "That's what I plan on doing, too." My father nodded and then he leaned down to place a kiss on my forehead. "I love you, get well baby." My parents shared a look before they wished me well and left. Great, now I was left alone to think and usually my thinking got me in trouble. I would have *thoughts* and those thoughts lead me down a path of loss of self worth. I didn't do a lot of thinking and it was mostly for my own good. The last time I thought...it wasn't pretty. Shrugging that off, I began to think of all the Black Eyed Peas songs I was in the mood for listening to. "Imma Be" maybe. Hmm, that was a good one. I had been rambling through the playlist when the door opened to reveal a worried looking Jerome. He was just standing at the threshold watching me with sad eyes. "You can come in if you want." He looked a little frantic when he shook his head. "I don't get it. You don't hate me? You're not mad?"

I frowned at that. "Wow. If I gave off that impression then I'm sorry—'cause I'm really not that nice." He nodded before he walked in and hesitantly over to me. He scratched his braids and said, "So, your insurance provider assured me that your name was Simone Randon. Am I wrong?"

I shook my head. "You're as right as you'll ever be."

He smiled and said, "Well, my name is Jerome Cooper. Don't worry; my insurance provider will pay for everything, so there's no need for court. Is there?" His eyes were hopeful and beseeching when I answered. "I really don't know dude. My dad is all over your ass." His eyes widened and he covered his face with his hands. "I am so grounded."

I rolled my eyes and said, "Hey, if you're nice enough I just might not press charges."

"Oh, God!" He groaned. "I'm sorry. Look if I—"

I laughed then; his nervousness was seriously humoring me. "You're funny, Cooper."

A small smile touched his lips when he explained, "I was on my way to pick my sister up from work when the car just sped out of control. The brakes stopped working and I thank Jesus that there was no one else in the road I could've hurt— though I am sorry for harming you, Simone."

I nodded, not really caring for what the dude had to say, when a thought occurred to me. "Cooper? As in Georgia Cooper's...*brother*?" His eyes narrowed suspiciously when he said. "Y-Yeah. How do you know...?" Realization struck him then and he clapped his hands in success. "You're not *that* Simone? The girl my sister has been talking about every day? No shit?" He offered his hand to me and said. "Well, it's nice to meet you. Sorry it's not under better circumstances though." I looked at his hand as if he was insane. He lowered it when he realized I wouldn't meet him halfway. "I'd shake your hand if mine didn't hurt so got-damn badly." I said the words bitterly and his eyes met mine, searing me. He licked his lips before saying, "I guess I deserve that one." He sighed, shrugged, and said finally. "Well, I just came here to apologize again. It was nice meeting you though." Before I could retort, he was out the door. I sighed. People *really* should stop leaving me to wallow in my thoughts, alone.

Chapter Four

SIT DOWN FOR YOUR RIGHTS

"ARE YOU OKAY SIM?" Seth shouted the second he burst through my bedroom door. It would be strange if we had not known each other for such a long time. Besides my dad, he was the only male condoned inside my room. Looking up at him I sighed, so not wanting to get into it right now. Seth was hovering over my bed and feeling every part of my body. It was not sexual or anything—just annoying. "Simone you were in an accident, were you not?"

I sighed, "It was on the news, wasn't it?"

"Hell yeah! Are you hurt?" I shrugged his roaming hands from my body and blew out a sharp breath in agitation. Seth shook his hair away from his eyes and said, "All right, I'm sorry, but you know I worry about you Sim."

I rolled my eyes at the trueness of his words. "True that. Sorry for being so testy—it's just that I don't like having a lot of attention drawn to me."

He nodded, "I understand, I just don't agree with you." Seth said the words tiredly and plopped down on my beanbag chair. His long legs made him look awkward sitting there in such a girly room. I swallowed and prepared myself for this battle I knew was imminent. "Seth, how many times do I have to remind you that I'm just not that pretty?"

His tone was warning, "Simone..."

I held my hand up to stop him. "No. You know that I'm hideous—hell, everyone does—yet you continue to be around me." My hand moved reflexively to my familiar love handles. I was frowning when I continued, "I just don't get you." I didn't look at him to read his expression; I already knew. I mean, the disappointment he was radiating was damn near tangible. There was silence for a moment, complete silence. Again, it made me think, which I never favored doing. Why was Seth by my side? After all these years, from the third grade to now, he was the only person to not judge me. To look me in the eyes and tell me that he truly

26

thought I was delusional whenever I put myself down. He thought I wasn't ugly, and to me, I thought that in the beauty department I seriously didn't make the cut. Seriously though, what did some gorgeous guy stay by a frumpy, tri-racial, nerd-girl's side for?

I mean—*gorgeous!*

I gritted my teeth, unable to stand the raw disgust I felt for myself. How could I be doing this? Questioning my friend's motives? My *best* and only friend? Shit, it was a wonder how he put up with me the times I did this.

Suddenly, a hand was there to caress my shoulder. The action didn't invoke any pain, but I was still a little sore from the car inci dent. I hadn't realized my eyes were shut until I pried them open and saw Seth, I mean really saw him, and discovered the pain there. His eyes were watering but he didn't dare allow his tears to fall because he was macho that way. Keeping his sad eyes on me, his hands trailed down from my shoulder to where my hands rested on my belly. "I thought I lost you today Simone." He looked pensive. "You're so beautiful...I can't even imagine living without you."

"Seth—"

He ducked his head down to place a kiss there and breathed tenderly, cautiously, "Baby, I wish you could see what I see." I was crying now and he leaned down from where he sat upon my bed and gently nipped the tears from my face. I sighed heavily, shut my eyes tight, slid down inside my covers and hid my face; the face that I apparently saw *way* differently from my best friend. I could feel his arms wound around me through the thick covers and I suddenly felt guilty and unworthy in his presence for some reason. Unable to contain myself, I blurted, "Just leave, Seth." His arm was gone instantly and I frowned at that. Expecting an argument, I sat up to steal a glance at him to be welcomed by the absence of my friend and the pregnant silence that he left behind.

My boss, thankfully, gave me the rest of the week off to recover from my oh-so traumatic run in with the ponderous Chevy-like object. Charlene Anders, my boss, was dramatic that way and very "save the world", so it was very easy to run game with her. Good thing I was not that sort of person—most days, anyway. I was lying in bed, home alone, bored as hell, watching a severely bad *Lifetime* movie. I couldn't recall the name of it, but involved loads of treachery and fornication between very odd groups of people. Victoria, the main character, cheated on her husband with a stranger only to find out that stranger was actually her long-lost brother. Torn over it, she decides to "woman-up" and confronts her husband, Tom, about it. However, as she's creeping through the house in search of him, she hears noises, opens a door and witnesses the shock of her life which was Tom having sex with their next door neighbor, Javier.

Victoria was scrambling around the house in search of her shotgun when my cell phone rang the tune, "Dirty Bit" by Black Eyed Peas, interrupting my movie. "Shit! Shit! Shit!" I hit the send button and barked, "What is it?"

"Momo?" It was Georgia. "I need your help." Her voice sounded grave, urgent, which was rare for her. I sighed impatiently and repeated, "What is it?"

"I *really* need you to come over!" She was sobbing now. "It's important." Unconvinced, I waved it away and said distantly, "Well, can it wait until Victoria—"

"Simone, somebody just shot my brother!" She screamed. "Help me! I don't know what to do…"

My heart sunk at the words. "W-What?"

"My parents are gone and I don't know what to do, oh God…" The line went dead and I knew where I was going next: wherever the hell Georgia Cooper lived.

"Damn it all!" I exclaimed as I sped down the busy street. I totally ditched my movie and was now on my way to 317 Fort Avenue, or Georgia's place. I snooped around her employee profile and discovered her personal information like her address and eye color and yada yada yada. "Ah!" I exclaimed when I nearly tore the door off an open car while I zoomed by. Damn, that would have been the second accident this week—talk about stress. My mother would have had my head, too, since this was her car. Obviously, mine was in the shop undergoing surgery. Even though my body was still half stiff and pained, I forged on and made my way down College Street, past Newark Drive, and finally reached Fort Avenue.

317 stood tall and refined smack dab in the middle of the neighborhood. It was apparently duplex and dark brown with polished woodwork and clean shutters. Even though it was a sweaty August afternoon, the house seemed to maintain its cool appeal with its cleanness and welcoming aura. Considering the circumstances it wasn't pretty to me and as I sloppily parked I dashed to the front porch. I banged on the door and yelled, "Georgia!" There was silence and so I kept screaming and making an ass out of myself to the public eye. This was actually one of the times I didn't

care what people thought, my trainee was in trouble. I could feel tears prick my eyes at the unfairness of it all—I couldn't reach her and she probably died of a heart attack from the stress of watching her brother being shot. Shoot, I would have. I gave the front door one final kick when I heard a strident wail from the upstairs.

Georgia!

"Georgia! Sweetie, are you okay? Open the door so we can call the police!" At the mention of the term, "police", I received many hostile glares from people passing by. Deciding to keep it to myself, I scanned my surroundings and found a gigantic stone. Did I dare? I marched over to the stone, picked it up and prepared to throw it until I heard a voice from behind me.

"Shut the hell up, Georgia!" The stone I was holding slipped from my hands and landed squarely on my foot. "Shit!" I screamed from pain and disbelief.

Jerome came running toward me in the same attire I last seen him in two days ago in the incident. His hair was out now and in a loose ponytail at the rear of his head. He was frowning when he said, "Why were crying and holding a stone poised at my front door?"

I was gasping from the pain and amazement of this situation. "Y-You're supposed to be...dead." He looked as if I was crazy. "Or at least hemorrhaging on the floor somewhere."

"What are you—?"

"Momo! You came!" Georgia's voice came excitedly from the doorway. She practically fluttered over to the front lawn to sit down on the grass next to me where I cradled my possibly fractured foot. Jerome was on the other side of me studying my face worriedly and finally saying, "Georgia, what the hell did you do?"

Georgia was unfazed by the hostility in his tone when she said, "Oh, I see you're home Jerome. That's awesome, 'cause I know I'll need a second opinion."

"For what?" He and I hollered in synchronization.

She looked as though she'd die from excitement when she answered, "My outfit for the first day of school!"

Chapter Five

Taking Deep Breaths Underwater

"You told her what?" Jerome yelled at his sister. Since my foot was totally out of whack, I had to wait until Jerome was finished chewing Georgia out before he could take me home. And, damn me, I left my wallet at home so I couldn't call a taxi. My parents were both hard at work and unreachable, and I refused to ask Jerome for anything. Instead, he wasn't taking no for an answer when he jacked my car keys and told me he was driving me home.

Or to a hospital...

I was lying vertically on the Cooper's living room couch with my foot propped on the end of it. It felt as if it was pulsating along to the tune of my throbbing

33

headache. And the sibling war was so not helping assuage the pain, too.

"Georgia, why must you make everyone believe this family is strange?"

Her voice was pleading, "I do not!"

"Yeah, you do." He sighed angrily, his accent thickened. "I come back from the gym to find your co-worker about to break the door down and you dragging our damn name through the mud." Jerome glared at her. "Thanks, sis."

"Come on Ro!" She was smiling, trying to appease him. "I'm sorry; I was just trying to—"

He held his hand up in dismissal. "I'm not the one you should be apologizing to—" he pointed in my direction. "Now you better hope she forgives you, because you're making it hard for *me*!" He stomped off to the back of the house and left the two of us alone.

"Georgia, you—" I began, but the tears in her eyes broke me. I'd prepared the whole thing in my head: I'd cuss her out, storm out, and never see her again. The little twit overdid it this time, and I really wasn't that nice a person to just up and forgive her for nearly breaking my foot. But the look she gave me turned my plans into mush and I wanted to cuss myself out for thinking such things. Jerome may do things that way, calling the child every name in the book and storming off, but I wasn't like that. I mean, seriously, she was only fifteen.

Georgia approached me gingerly until the silence made me think, so to avoid it I spoke, "Just- Just show me the darn outfit Georgia."

Her eyes lit up at the mention of her ulterior motive for my visit. "Really? You're not mad, Momo?"

I glared daggers at the freshman, "Hell yeah I'm still mad! But I'm here now, so show me before I get any more upset."

"Yays!" She chirped and flung herself over me. Even though she was skinny, I could still feel the weight of her bones. I hissed in pain when Jerome's voice broke the laughter in the air. "You're *hurting* her, Georgia." He just sounded resigned and sort of sad as she stood and looked at me uneasily before saying, "Um, s-sorry, Simone. I'll just be going now..." She ran upstairs all depressed again. He sighed before trudging over to me and sitting down on the empty space near my foot. "I don't know what to do with her sometimes, I swear. It's like she makes it a point to piss me off any way she can." When his eyes found mine I couldn't help but blurt, "She's only fifteen. Give her a break."

Jerome scratched his hair and said tiredly, "Well, I would if she deserved it." He rubbed his hands over his face and said lowly, "You ready to get out of here?" More than ever, was what I started to say, but remembered what Georgia wanted to show me. He helped me sit up on the couch and I said, "Hey, um, can I just check her outfit? I mean, she went to all the trouble—"

"No!" He grabbed my wrists and pinned me to the cushion so we were face-to-face. Jerome's face was dark red when he said, "Just listen to me for *once!* Gosh, you're even more annoying than my sister." My eyes were rounded with fear and I began to lash back when I actually thought about my disadvantages. He was way stronger than me, my foot wasn't fully functioning, and even if I did run I wouldn't make it far considering the fact that he had my car keys.

Breathing hard, I gasped from the pain he was causing my wrists. "Okay! Just get off of me!" He smiled devilishly when he looked down to where our chests contacted. My ragged breaths made my chest heave quickly causing them to rub up against him. His grip loosened when he stood and helped me up. I lost balance on my damaged foot and fell into his strong arms. "Oh, I'm so sorry I forgot." Biting his lip, he bent down and scooped me into his arms, cradling me in a gentle embrace. When he reached the front door, he shifted my weight into his left arm so he could unlock and open it. When we were outside, he carried me methodically to my car, strapped me inside the passenger seat, and got in. I was surprised by so many things, including the fact he could carry me without protest, and the mood swing.

"Where do you live?" He asked gently.

My words were clipped, "East Ninth Street."

"Okay." He started the car and moved easily down the road. I directed him where to go until we reached a large white house with a huge lawn and flowers sprouting everywhere around it. I would have been embarrassed had he not scared me so badly. I told him where to park and from then on we just sat there, in silence. The silence made me think and this time I spoke a thought aloud, "What the hell was that?"

A tic started in his jaw when he answered in a soft voice, "I'm sorry, I overreacted. That was very wrong of me—"

Warranting death, I leaned over and punched him in the jaw.

Scared of what he might've done, I fumbled with my door to have him lay a gentle hand on my arm. I stopped and turned to look at him. His eyes were sad when he said, "I'm not a bad person, Simone. Just let me explain something to you." His voice shifted to matter-of-fact. I frowned and recoiled to the farthest corner away from him. Jerome seemed to be relaxed as he laid back and stared out through the windshield. He looked like one of those serial killers that planned and thought things through—a methodical one. This was the craziest shit in my life though; I just met this guy and already he was tweaking out on me. I rolled my eyes; that was just my luck.

"What do you want from me?" I asked through gritted teeth. What was this, give-the-fat-girl-a-heart-attack day? He chuckled darkly and said, "All of you, actually." I frowned as his eyes lingered in areas that made uncomfortable. What the fuck was going on? I cowered away when he said, "Do you wear glasses Simone?"

The question was so off topic and casual I found myself answering anyway, "Yeah." I watched him suspiciously, "Why?"

Jerome licked his lips before answering, "And on the night of the accident, when everyone blamed me for 'skidding across the road in front of you' were you wearing them?"

I thought back to that night and realized the trueness of his accusation. I remembered telling Georgia how much I hated them that night. She wanted me to show her a closer look, so I handed them to her and forgot to get them back. Shit, he was right, but no way was I going to admit that. "I remember it being dark out, yes."

His smile was filled with malice, "Mm-hm, and if that's true, then I can legally toss out that lawsuit your father's throwing at me and file this new evidence I so casually collected." He dug around in his pocket and pulled out a black case that held my glasses inside them. He waved them in my face and I reached for them only to have him snatch them away. "Until I have what I want, you can have these back." Jerome waggled the case again.

"I hate you!" I spat.

He only smiled and winked at me. "Thanks babe—hate only makes what I'm offering much more fun." Jerome laughed maniacally. I shook my head in disbelief, "Who are you?"

"It's quite simple really," he began, ignoring my question. "I want that lawsuit lifted to clear my name and you're going to tell daddy to do just that, or else." I felt like I was in one of those bad Lifetime movies. *Or else...*

"Or else what?" I demanded.

Jerome sighed, "I did a little digging around and found some interesting information about your father, Mr. Zachary Randon."

My heart sunk. No way... "Shut up. You don't know what you're talking about."

He laughed out loud. "God, your anger turns me on!" He winked before continuing. "Remember the Shay's Case three years ago?"

"The what?" I didn't think I heard him correctly. It couldn't be...

He nodded, "Oh, don't play dumb Simone. We all know your father's a murderer..." His brows rose and I leaned over to hit him again when his expression stopped me. His expression was completely feral. There was only three people who knew the truth about that case—my parents and I. That was such a sad case...such a sad week...how could this asshole just...?

"You monster- you wouldn't!" I was sobbing now; there was terror behind that case.

"But I will." There was a strange glint in his eyes that told me he was serious, but was using dark humor. Sitting there thinking again, I considered my options. He told the glasses tale. Who cares? All I'd do was pay a fine, and so would he still. But if I didn't do what he

40

wanted...and he told the truth behind the Shay's case to the world...

I did not even want to think of that gritty outcome.

Swallowing my pride I repeated, "What do you want from me?"

Jerome smiled a smile so evil and tempestuous I had to turn away, feeling visually violated.

He chuckled. "Sex."

I had to do a double take on that one. Did he just demand sex from me? *Me?* I shook my head. "No way."

He cackled. "Aw, is the little baby *abstaining?*"

I glared at him. Actually I was, but I did not mention it. He probably would have wanted this more. Resisting the urge to punch him in the face I said, "Just tell me the terms you're proposing and *maybe* we could renegotiate." My voice was strong, and I was glad, because I was feeling all sorts of weak right then.

Jerome grabbed me by the hair, jerked me toward him and delivered a hungry, yet way too professional, kiss on my lips. When he jerked me back, I thought I was seeing stars for a moment, and then I composed myself. He brushed off his clothes and continued on as if that hadn't happened. "A month of your time is what

I want. Agree to thirty days of straight sex—on call and whenever I want it— and your dirty little secret on the Shay's case will be yours to keep."

Chapter Six

A raBID GOriLLa

"I'll give you until school starts for an answer, okay?" Jerome said flippantly after helping me limp to my doorstep. I protested and complained the entire journey though. His mood swings were throwing me off, and as I turned to give him a piece of my mind he was already a vague figure down the street. I was so pissed I could have spat needles, but instead I was clutching my house and car keys so tightly my palms bled. I wiped the blood on my sweater and unlocked the door to stagger inside my house. Once the door was shut, and locked, I walked as fast as I could to the purple room, which was the reading room, and sat down at the computer. My foot was hurting too badly to make it upstairs to my laptop, so I had to make do with the closest object with internet access.

School was in two days and I had to work fast and make sure that I had as much evidence of the Shay's case destroyed. Surprisingly enough, there was a folder sitting in the recycle bin that had been there for almost four years now. I didn't bother to open it and reread the horrible truth, so I highlighted it and any other folder lying about with name Shay's on it, and permanently trashed them. Still paranoid, I Google'd anything else revealing too much of the case. I checked local news sites, Wikipedia, the *Washington Post*, the *New York Times*...everywhere seemed to explain only a fraction of the truth and/or the story we distributed to the public. I sighed in relief; there was nothing too raw to lead anyone onto the truth. So how the hell could Jerome, a new guy in town, know about it? My mind was racing and I was retracing all my steps from this week. Okay, so I went to work, came home. I went to work, get in a car incident, went to the hospital, and went home. Wednesday, or today, I wake up, watch a movie, go to Georgia's house, and then all of this happened. What the hell did this guy want with me? Me? "*Agree to thirty days of straight sex and your dirty little secret on the Shay's case will be yours to keep...*" Why would he blackmail me that way? I mean, all he had to do was ask me to ask my father to repeal the lawsuit and it would have been done. End of story.

But no, he just had to go and threaten me to get what he wanted.

And with the Shay's Case? That was just a low blow. Thinking back, I tried to remember the...emotions of that day. The day the judge deemed the case over with and the shame I felt, so profoundly, for my father. I believe, on that day I lost an incredible amount of respect for him. He was just so obsessed with winning that case and getting our family out of our financial hole that he went to unprecedented lengths...*illegal* lengths...

"Simone? Baby, are you feeling better?" My mother's concerned voice echoed from the front door.

It scared the crap out of me and I yelped, "Y-Yes mom?"

The sound of her footsteps reverberated throughout the silent house as she walked inside the purple room to smile at me. "Oh, I see that some of the swelling went down, thank the lord!" She hurried over to me and studied my face. Her eyes then shifted to the computer screen. "What do you have there?" My hands fumbled with mouse until it reached the exit icon and turned the computer off. "N-Nothing, mom. Um—"

"Was that...please tell me you weren't snooping around in your father's files again, Simone how many times must you—"

"Mom! It was a homework assignment, chill." Her face was all flushed and I knew she was riled. Ever since that case, she was always persistent of me not even breathing the word, 'court'.

Her eyes were guarded for a moment before she cleared her throat and asked, "So you made it to your doctor's appointment?"

Damn, I swear I was battling teenage Alzheimer's. "Um, yeah. Yes, I did." Okay, so I fibbed a little, sue me. What else would I tell her? "*Oh, sorry mom, I forgot. Instead I went over to a friend's house, broke my foot, and was threatened by this stalker guy into making me have sex with him. Other than that, I still think I'm hideous. So h ow was your day?*"

She waved her hand, urging me to continue. "Uh-huh, and what did he say? Did he give you any more medicine or...?"

I shook my head vigorously, "Nope. I'm as fit as a fiddle."

She looked uncertain before nodded and began toward the cooking quarters. "Oh. Okay. Are you hungry?" I heard my stomach growl and shook it off. No way did I need any more food—I was big enough. "N-No. I just finished eating when you came home." The look she gave me was skeptic. "Simone...?"

My stomach lurched at the smell of last night's dinner she was nuking in the microwave. I resisted the urge to tackle it, and stood cautiously on my hurt foot. I winced at the pressure and sure enough she noticed, "I'm fine."I said brokenly from the pain. She started toward the purple room when I said, "I dropped my chemistry book on my foot and it hurts like heck now. I'm fine mom." I managed a smile and limped up the stairs.

When I reached my room, I collapsed on my king sized bed and closed my eyes. I was in another world right then, a world of peace and no pain. I imagined that I was thin and had the hottest boyfriend at my side and Rachel and I were friends again. I breathed lightly and a warm smile spread across my face from the vision. I wanted it to be true so bad I could cry, but I didn't feel that mushy-gushy at the moment. The vision started off as heavenly and surreal and suddenly transitioned into a maniacal laugh and darkness. It was cold and the only words that were being repeated were, "We all know your father's a murderer..."

Tears were falling down my face at the mere thought of having to even repeat the name of that case. Again, I saw my father's depleted face as I watched him with utter disgust. I sighed; words couldn't describe how much I hated thinking...

"How's your steak, Simone? Is it too rare for you?" My mother asked me later that night at dinner. My father looked up from his plate with curious eyes. "Yeah, sweetheart, all you've been doing is poking at it? Is it that terrible?"

I frowned. "No, it's okay. I'm just not hungry."

"Well, all right then." He straightened his back, yawned, and stood from his chair. His eyes slid lazily over to my mom. "Well, babycakes that was one good meal."

She blushed. "Why, *gracias Senior Randon*." They exchanged sly glances at each other before he sat his plate in the sink, rinsed it, and sauntered upstairs. My mother's eyes devouring him by every step he took. I sighed; did they think I didn't know what just happened? "Mom?"

Her eyes were fixated on the stairs dad went toward. "Hmm?" She answered distantly.

"I'm finished eating. You can give my leftovers to the street dogs or whatever it is you do with them."

She came out of her trance and cast a worried gaze my way. "But baby you barely touched—"

"I'm fine!" I snapped. Jeez, was she getting it?

She frowned then and gave me a hard stare. "Use that tone one more time and I'll sit here and make sure you eat every crumb off that plate, understood?"

Of course, she just had to be difficult. I stood and took my plate to the fridge. "Yes mom."

"Good. Now go to your room."

I took her advice and headed upstairs.

When I reached my bed I sat down and turned my TV on. Sigh, there was nothing on, and I wasn't in the mood to watch a movie. Well, maybe I'd record a *Lifetime* movie and watch it later, but right now I had another thought in mind. I decided against using the house phone, because I knew my parents didn't really trust me since the last time they left me to think too long and by myself. It ended horribly, and I honestly didn't blame them for the supervision. So I took my cell phone off the charger and swam around in my contacts and pressed CALL on the person I wanted to talk to in forever.

There was a dial tone, but she answered on the third ring. "Simone?" She asked hesitantly.

I grinned goofily at the sound of one of my favorite cousin's voice. "Luz? Hey! I was just calling to see how you were doing. We haven't spoken in a while." Her voice automatically grew as loud and wild as she was. "OMG, you're so right! We miss you here in Queens girl, how you doin'? When you gonna' visit?"

"Oh." I said uneasily. Why didn't I expect her to ask that? "Well, I'll try to come over some time uh..."

"Oh, it's all right. I know school just started and it was rude of me to ask that of you..." Her tone had shifted into accusing and it threw me off. Frowning I said, "Oh come on now! You're making me feel bad." I sighed. She really was.

"Well, you should!" Luz said jokingly. "We've been tight for, like, ever, and you still can't visit a homegirl? It's been two years, Mo."

I smiled and fidgeted with my fingers. "I know, I'll be there." I said then added quietly, "One day."

Luz answered loudly, which was just Luz. "Oh! So it's like that, huh? I got you..." Her voice transcended into a plea. "Come on! Don't you love us—your family? My mom has been asking about you, like, nonstop. She was just worried about you after...you know."

"Yeah." I answered distantly. I think we all knew what she was talking about. The time people gave me too much time to think to myself. Well, I over thought, and ended up constantly supervised. "I know."

"Well, everything's good here though. I'm just planning the family reunion and other stuff. My god daughter is getting so big! Oh, I am so gonna send you some pictures of Yazzy." Her tone shifted to accusing. "But, I wouldn't have to if you would come up here and see for yourself."

"I'm sorry, I will." I said reassuringly, knowing just how emotional she could be at times. I totally forgot about the stupid family reunion. Every few years my entire family met somewhere in New York and we'd sing and dance and fight, etc. Funny how I happened to call when that event was coming up. Oh, and Jasmine, or Yazzy, was Luz's best friend's baby. Well, she was about a year and a half now and Luz absolutely adored her. I believed she was moved out of her parent's house by now, but I hadn't seen them in two years. Reina and I were cool, and she was still really tight with Luz since they've met a few years ago. "So..." I said, pondering the next subject in silence. "Do you still have a crush on that guy—uh, what's his name—Jacob?"

Luz sighed in exasperation, "His name's Joseph. We're dating now, Simone."

I widened my eyes at that. I remembered she had this, like, psycho crush on him a while back, and I also knew that he thought she was just some loud, crazy, girl who wouldn't leave him alone. Huh, I guess things really had changed since the last time I visited there. "You know, if you just called to give me a bad day, then can you just spare me and hang the hell up?"

Now that set me off. "Listen here broad, I just called in to say hello and to see how you were doing. But if you wanna get all *emotional*—"

"Simone, really, it's not that serious. So shut the hell up, settle the hell down, and bring your ass to Queens next weekend." Her tone was casual, as if she was discussing the weather or something.

I sucked my teeth at that. "Luz—"

"Okay, so it's settled. Love ya bitch—kisses!" Then she hung up after making kissing sounds.

"Ugh!" I exclaimed and fell back on my bed, a little pissed.

Chapter Seven

Seeking Chocolate During Rush Hour

I had to swallow my pride to do this one. It was never my thing to *apologize to anyone or* for anything. I've always had the logic of, "if you don't like it—then forget you." However, I knew my limits and I knew Seth's and I knew I excelled them. Gosh, it sucked when I had to do this.

I pulled over on the curb outside his family's apartment building—the Washington apartments. Seth lived on the first floor, 4A, and I was thankful for it, because everyone knew fat girls didn't like to travel harsh distances. I adjusted my bulgy sweater, squinted from the sun, and continued to his front door. I figured that he would be home even though it was a

Sunday afternoon and he could be at the skate park. His mother, Gloria, was big on the first day of school and fresh starts which was why I knew she was in there experimenting new clothes on Seth and her other eleven year old son, Cody. Cody, however, was a mean little devil who sullied any and every piece of clothing his mother bought him. She was a single mother, since their father died of a heart attack when Cody was three and Seth ten, and she never liked to extravagantly spend her money. I mean, she worked in a nursing home and made an adequate amount, but for her to spend extra was financially crippling and morally unnecessary.

Sighing deeply, I knocked lightly on the door and waited, allowing the suspense to eventually kill me. A tall woman answered the door at that moment and suddenly I felt very small. She stood at a whopping six feet with waist length hair that was as black as coal. Her face was juvenile despite the subtle streaks of gray in her hair. She wore a short orange sundress and her smile was radiant.

She waved at me and that's when Seth appeared abruptly behind her. Seth felt his mother's shoulder then, and signed for her to go back inside the house. She smiled and did just that.

Oh yeah, I never mentioned that Gloria was deaf.

I understood what they were saying because Seth taught me when I was real young. I first met Seth in the third grade, and I always remembered the tall lady that would pick him up every day and use these exotic hand signs. What baffled me was how Seth understood, and then it fascinated me into learning it.

When Gloria was gone, I signed to a frowning Seth, "*I'm sorry.*"

He just stood up there and smirked down at me. Rolling his eyes and tossing his hair out of them he responded, "*Have you came to your senses, Sim?*"

"Yes!" I exclaimed out loud in a hurry.

Seth shut the door behind him and we were now alone in the hallway. Then he drew closer to me. *Way* closer to me. I *so* wanted to sigh at my best friend's touchy feely personality. Yeah, that was how he expressed how he felt, by touching. Sigh, especially me though. When I'd become angry he'd stroke my hair or place his hands on my shoulders. I guess he had to be that way though; after all, his mom mainly relied on sight and touch to communicate. Huh, quite the son she had.

"So you have?" He said, looking down at me with eyes filled with so much emotion. Mostly pain and...lust? I wondered what he desired though—that kind of confused me. His hands found my shoulders and he leaned down to whisper directly in my face, "Prove it."

My heart was racing from the contact, and I was a little breathless when I said, "What do you mean?"

He ran his hand through my straightened hair and the smirk was still on his face when he answered. "Prove to me that you believe you're beautiful."

I waved that away and stood further back. "N-No, I'm not. You know that." He gave me a look and I restated more firmly. "I'm not pretty."

He shrugged. "Well, I guess that's what you think then. Later." Seth turned around and had his hand on the knob when I rushed him and held his tall frame from behind. "NO! Okay, okay, I'll prove it." Having Seth angry at me was like torture. Mostly because he was a natural born master at the silent treatment.

The asshole had a knack for making people feel guilty. "I'm sorry, I swear." He turned around in my arms and, with his bony self, lifted me off my feet to kiss me quickly on the forehead. When he put me down I looked at him, bewildered, and sputtered, "H-How did you just—"

He placed a finger to my lips and shook his head.

I rolled my eyes; I was really tired of guys doing that to me. "The first day of school." I said quickly, before I could change my mind. "Tomorrow."

Seth frowned in confusion, apparently not understanding. "Tomorrow?"

I nodded, "Yes. I will wear something completely...un...Simone-like. I'll be...*comfortable with my body image.*" I said in a very counselor-like tone. He smiled and cupped my cheek gently in his palm. "I don't want you to be what you're not...I don't want you to be uncomfortable—" I put my hand on his chest and looked into his eyes. His cheeks reddened at the action and he stopped talking. "Oh, Sim..." His voice was dreamy and it made me a little uneasy so I continued on with my plan. "Just for one day, I'll show you that—that I'm not...*displeased* with how I...how I look."

Seth smiled and said finally, "I believe in you, babe."

Gosh, I was really glad that I wasn't limping anymore. It was mostly because I would look like a retard for the first day of school wearing what I intended to wear. So, it was off to the mall I went. I made that promise on

58

the spot to Seth and now, unfortunately, I had to back it up.

I pulled in to the parking lot of Macy's and got out. My mother had such a dear heart for allowing me to use her car for a few days. I knew it was different for her to travel every day to work with my father. They loved each other dearly, but I knew my mom just loved her space and she wasn't a very nice morning person.

Anyways, when I walked inside the store I caught sight of the aisle I wanted and rushed it. I chose a white fitting shirt and dug around a little for the right pair of pants. After a considerable amount of uneasy stares at my current attire, I finally settled on three pairs of skinny jeans—black, light gray, and brown—and three matching shirts for them. I decided on a flaring tan shirt for the brown jeans; the white fitting shirt and a black cardigan to go over it for the black jeans, and for the gray jeans I chose a white tee that read, Simply Me, on the front with gray and pink letters. To match all that I picked out I found some earrings, handbags, and flats. "Okay, I'm done now." I said to myself and headed for the checkout aisle. As I waited in line I caught sight of a dark purple sundress that was sort of low cut and knee length. It was ruffled from the waist up and required a mini jacket to cover the back. It was probably the most beautiful dress I'd ever saw. "You'd look wonderful in that, you know?" Came a meek voice from behind me. When I turned around, I saw a black girl about my height with her hair up in a ponytail that hung just past her neck. She was actually kind of pretty in a non homosexual way and weighed just about as much as me. "Excuse me?" I asked, on guard.

Her eyes were kind and filled with laughter, "Oh, I was just saying. You were practically drooling."

I eyed her suspiciously and shrugged. "So, you think I should get it?"

She nodded vigorously, "Absolutely."

After giving her another doubtful onceover, I walked slowly toward the loveliness and ran my fingers over it. It was smooth, and expensive, I could tell. I practically groaned from the pleasure of the softness and the anticipation of having it on my skin. Why the hell not? I mean, I deserved some sort of treat for what I would have to face later. And Jerome and the Shay's case didn't slip my mind—I would have to get my hands dirty one of these days, I just didn't know when. And there was no way I could ever agree to what Jerome even offered, like I was some common whore he could use for his sexual experiments. Besides, I was saving my little piece of purity for my soon-to-be husband. And frankly, Jerome didn't make the cut.

"It's pretty, huh?" The girl asked--- zapping me out of my deep thinking (thank God!).

I turned to her so quickly I nearly gave myself whiplash. "Uh, y-yes." I rubbed my neck, carefully took down the dress, and made my way to the check-out line. "Thanks for holding my spot in line...um?" I probed for a name.

"Prudence Alcott, but you can call me Pru." She held her hand out to me. "Nice to meet you...?"

"Oh, um, you can call me Simone." I eyed the jeans folded on her forearm and smiled appreciatively. "Hm, you've got taste. I like those."

Her eyes followed my gaze and she smiled in realization at the pants. "Oh, thanks! I've had to...it was just a climb to get them. I've been dying to get these." Her voice was so full of affection that I could tell that she didn't come by things she wanted so easily. I nodded while I watched her, gaining a respect for the girl and knowing how weird it was to give that out to a complete stranger.

It was my turn to pay; I did, and started for the door. I sighed; it was so refreshing to get home at once. My hand was on the door when a whining voice stopped me. "I'm sorry ma'am, but you need another dollar to get this item."

"Oh, come on! A dollar? Do you have *any* idea how long I've been penny pinching to get these?"

The whiny woman was persistent. "These jeans are forty dollars, ma'am. If you fail to provide proper compensation, then you must return the item or I will call security." Her voice was whiny and boring, but still thickly laden with warning. My back turned, I debated with myself for a full minute.

It was Pru.

I mean, the girl did help me out with my body makeover for tomorrow. The least I could do was spot her a buck. "Listen here lady; I have kids to raise—"

"Hey miss?" I called out to the cashier lady as I advanced toward her. Pru watched me like a deer caught in the headlights for a moment before she realized what I was doing. "No, I'm fine Simone. You really don't have to—"

I held my hand up to silence her while I handled it. I wagged an unpainted fingernail in the old cashier lady's face. She frowned. "Miss, whoever you are, I don't want you to ever mistreat this girl again." My voice was dead calm. "Trust me, if you do, I'd have every got-damn clothing store aware of you, and you'd be unhappily unemployed. My father knows some important people who could easily—"

Pru's hand was on my arm now, she squeezed it firmly while saying, "I'm fine, but thank you. I'll just put the jeans back..."

I reached into my pocket and retrieved my wallet. I took out my father's gold card and handed it to the old wench. "For the jeans." She took the card with a shaking hand and handed me the receipt. "H-Have a n-nice day, ma'am." She looked frightened but I didn't care. The old hag. "Hope the rest of yours is exactly what you get as well, Miss." I took the card, put it back in my wallet, and was outside in an instant.

Jeez, I was getting soft.

Chapter Eight

TYING THE KNOT WITH BLOODY KNUCKLES

It was the morning of school when I realized something: Georgia. I'd promised to pick her up for the first day of school. And, shoot, I may be lazy and a little mean at times, but no way was I one to back down on my word. So I rolled out of bed and ran into the bathroom, hopped into the shower and washed. After my shower, I dried and flat ironed my hair. Well, I had natural curls, but I didn't like to wear them. It was much easier to just straighten it and be on my way. Ha, sort of like today. Even though it was the first day of school and the beginning of many people's excitement, I just wasn't that happy. And why the heck should I be? Deciding not go into the ramifications of my already cloudy day, I dried off and wrapped the towel around my body to begin sorting through my new clothes. Smiling, I decided to wear the purple dress that beckoned me in the mall yesterday. Thinking of that dress actually made me think of Prudence. I wondered what she was doing right then, and for some reason, if she was all right. It was never in my character to question someone's well being, so thinking of it anyway scared me.

Shaking away the bad feeling I had about her I slipped easily into the dress and just looked at myself in the mirror. For a good ten minutes I just stood there and relished in the splendid reflection smiling at me. Her dark hair was long, side-parted, and straightened past her elbows. The fitting, yet loose, dress fit her body like a second skin and she was also wearing purple hooped earrings. The shoes on her feet were violet flats that made the outfit more exotic. Her thin, black, mini jacket even made the girl look about ten pounds thinner.

I sighed; damn I was lucky that that girl was me.

"I'm ready now." I said over and over to myself so I wouldn't chicken out and jump back in bed. I had to woman up on this one, and that meant using tolerance. I went into the kitchen and grabbed a bowl of cereal. When I reached for the Lucky Charms, however, a few things happened. The first, I thought of that Black Eyed Peas song called "Shut Up" to calm my nerves, and the second thing, my cell phone began to vibrate in my purse (yes, I know, girly isn't it?). Realizing that it could be one of my parents, I ran for it and saw that it was a text message. I sat down at the kitchen counter then, and hovered over my bag reading what the text said:

> Got ur numba frm Georgia— so what's it gonna be?? I need an answer by 2day, plz. ;)

I wanted to bellow out in rage at that point. I was making it a habit to avoid the asshole, as well as the situation. How could he expect me to go along with a plan like that? No way—I couldn't even think about doing it. Harming myself, again, my family and everyone else that's helped me along the road. That would be a major slap in the face and defiling. I really had thought about asking Seth to help get me out of the bind, but remembered that that would involve letting another person know the truth behind the Shay's case. I exhaled slowly, trying to calm myself and avoid slamming my fist into a wall. I could feel tears prick my eyes but I blank them away. I had to be strong. I had to be a woman. I had to woman-up, and crying wasn't it. So, gathering all my strength and whatever dignity I had left, I picked up my phone and typed back to Jerome:

CAVE

ME: Okay…I'm in.

Chapter Nine

Reveling Shadows in Comatose

"Yay! You're here!" Georgia sprinted to my car when I pulled up at her house at eight in the morning. I unlocked the passenger door and she got in and buckled up. We sat there for a minute and I studied her outfit frowning. She wore a white tank top with a pair of white Capri's and white flats. Her micros were also done up in a ponytail and tied together with a white ribbon. Her earrings were studs, and she was also wearing clear and white bangles. "What?" She asked innocently. Shrugging, she began to dig around in her cream colored backpack and I commented, "Well, if you're looking for your white lipstick, you might want to rethink it—you'll look like a crack head."

Georgia placed a hand to her lips and said, "Well, I asked if you could approve my outfit or not, and you didn't!"

"Why didn't you ask your mom?" I knew there had to be someone in that house with a fashion sense.

She looked about embarrassed. "Well, she said it was adorable, so I listened." Georgia rolled her eyes and asked helplessly, "Could you come with me back in the house to try other stuff on? Please?"

I sighed and thought for a *really* long time. No way did I want to go in there and face that asshole of a brother of hers. "Georgia, no. There's no time. You look fine, let's just go."

"But Momo—" She began.

"No! Seriously dude, we're running late." I started the engine and drove down the street. We drove for a while in silence until Georgia broke it.

"Hey, um, Momo. Can I say something?"

I gritted my teeth. "Don't push me Georgia."

She held her hands up in surrender, "No. I was just going to say that you look really pretty. Your hair looks way better straight than frizzy." Now, I would've been offended had someone else said it, but it was only Georgia. I knew she would never say anything in meanness. That just wasn't her.

"Thanks, I guess." I said.

"You're very welcome." She said finally. The school, North Creston High, came into view and as we neared it Georgia began squealing. "Ah! Is this the school? Oh my gosh!"

"Settle down, freshman." I said nonchalantly as I pulled in to the student parking lot. There were hundreds of kids scattered around the lot, the building and the inside. It was a warm morning so everyone was showing skin. It was funny how I smiled at the thought of seeing Seth again. I had no idea why, but I felt proud that I was doing something, for once, to make *him* smile. Growing up, it was always him being the one to lighten the mood and cheer me up. And I was the depressing one who everyone had to keep a "watch" over. But it wasn't my fault, people just gave me too much time to think.

"Can I get out now?" Georgia asked anxiously. I hadn't realized we'd been sitting there in silence for the past few minutes. We probably looked mutant to the rest of the students eyeballing us. I shrugged, "Go ahead."

"Yay! I love you Momo!" She leaned over to hug me, I returned it and she opened the passenger door to get out. Before she shut the door she leaned down and said without emotion, "Oh and Jerome said to tell you, 'at one o' clock today'. Whatever that means." At that, she shut the door and fluttered inside—returning to her own bliss.

My heart was beating wildly at what she said. Okay, breathe. Breathe. That's all I had to do, get a hold on myself, and suck it up like a woman. When I was out of the car, I put my backpack on and held my purse like a lifeline. I was clenching and unclenching my fists by the time I walked inside the building and into the crowds full of lustful stares. I blushed from the unwanted attention and scurried along toward the bulletin board to check where my homeroom was. My finger skimmed through the long list of seniors until I finally found the R's. Randon: room 613. I frowned, trying to remember who's classroom it was and if I liked the teacher or not. The crowd's eyes shifted from desire to curiosity to astonishment. "Is that Simone?" I heard someone ask when I walked by.

"Why, yes it is." A deep voice answered, sort of dazed. It actually sounded as if the voices were following me to my homeroom. Feeling slightly creeped out I kicked my chubby little legs faster and sooner than I thought

I was at 613. Before I walked in though, the deep voice whispered closely to my ear, "Damn girl—you lookin' some kind of sexy!"

"What the—" I began to cuss the fool out when I finally turned around and stared up in astonishment at who it was. His hair was clipped from his eyes and combed back and sort of spiked. I could tell he was going for the Latin look- and damn, he rocked it. His clothes weren't skater punk like usual, but formal. He was wearing black slacks and a suit shirt with a tie and vest. Huh, and I just noticed the light mustache forming on his upper lip that only added to his appeal. I mean, the guy looked like sex on a platter.

Seth adjusted his tie and chuckled at my expression. "I look that bad?"

"I, uh, well—huh?" I was stuttering, which was odd for me. Seth kept his cool though and said, "You're so cute when you're flustered, Sim. That's a good look for you." He looped his arm through mine and we walked inside the classroom. There were only about three students in there at the moment even their gazes were loaded with amazement, matching the teacher's.

"So," Seth began when I sat at a desk at the back of the classroom. He sat on the desk before mine to talk to me standing up. "Um, what are you doing after school today?"

"Noth—" I began, but thought better of it. Of course, I'm only shaming myself this afternoon to protect my father from going to prison. Jeez, the love of a daughter. "I-I have something else planned for today. Sorry." I felt like shit when his features automatically went south and I wanted nothing more than to hold him. Standing there, making that sullen face, he reminded me of the adorable little dark-haired eight-year old boy I fell in love with. It was a cute expression, despite the glumness of it. Instinctively, his hand reached out to me and he started to fiddle with my hair. It was an idle gesture, but even that made me feel like a terrible friend for denying him.

Suddenly he nodded as if he solved something in his head and said, "With someone else?" his voice gruff with emotion, his face contrite. My eyes widened when I realized what he was talking about and how correct he'd been. I just couldn't tell him that. "Yes, my mother, as a matter of fact."

He nodded, not meeting my eyes. "I understand."

I opened my mouth to reschedule or at least talk it out when the bell rang. "Seth, maybe we can do somethi ng...later?"

He shrugged and a sad smile touched his lips, "Sure."

"Okay then. Well, I'll see you in third period." He nodded once more before he went out the door. Gosh, I was so damn tired of feeling like the bad guy. I shouldn't have to explain myself to him or anyone else. I could handle myself perfectly fine—except when people leave me to think.

That's when things get out of hand.

I was in second period when I felt something hit the back of my head. Putting a cap on my temper, I ignored it and resumed listening to Mrs. White's, my English IV teacher, lesson. We were just getting into the history of Transcendentalism when I heard a fierce hiss from behind me. The old Simone would have just pounced on whoever that was while jamming to a Black Eyed Peas song in her head. Yeah, and I was really considering reverting to my old ways until, as usual, the bell rang and the class emptied. When my things were gathered, I tossed my hair back and started for the door. "Simone!" Some girl said from behind me. It was familiar, but annoying, so I turned and snapped, "What?"

Prudence held her hand up and said hurriedly, "Sorry! I was trying to get your attention all period—here." She extended a folded piece of paper out to me and on the front of the page it read, My Number. I frowned, but took it.

So, that was her doing all that to get my attention. Well, she was lucky I didn't whip her ass, because I really wasn't that nice. I probably would have gained some sense though, because after all she was one of those people I wanted to save for some reason. It wasn't sympathy that I had for the girl, because it wasn't. Having that would make me no better a person, because how could I sympathize for somebody when I didn't even like myself? I empathized with her though—I could relate to the, "penny pinching" and saving your money for only the things you need. Before the Shay's case, my family was under the poverty line. Ever since then, I'd learned to appreciate more, because I knew just how quickly luxury could slip away.

I turned to look at her and smiled. "Hey, girl! I didn't know you were in this class! Heck, I didn't know you even went to this school." Looking down I noticed she was wearing the jeans I'd helped her get the other day. Pru scratched her braids before saying, "Yeah. Um, I just wanted to thank you for the other day—you didn't have to do that. I mean, I have a job and I could've found another dollar somewhere—"

I held my hand up. "You're very welcome. Don't mention it—it'll only annoy me."

She nodded quickly and frowned, "Okay, consider it done. But I still want to repay you somehow."

"Pru—"

"No. It'll annoy *me* if I don't repay you somehow. I don't like handouts, but mutual offerings I can deal with. So, how 'bout dinner?"

Jeez. Was it national, "Ask Simone out Day"? First Jerome, then Seth, now Pru. Damn, I was only one person. Sooner or later I would have to make an agenda for all of this. I sighed, knowing and understanding the undying pride within the girl. "Sure, why not? I'll be free..." I had to think about it. It was Friday now, and then I'd dedicate Saturday to Seth so Sunday was the best day I could think of. "...Sunday."

She hugged me and said, "Done."

When I was out the door I noticed that she'd been trailing me. I stopped and turned. "Are you following me?"

She laughed, "No, I'm going to room 804 Chemistry for third period. Where are you going?" I had no idea what was funny, but I laughed too. When I recovered I answered, "The same place as you. Come on." I gestured for her to walk beside me and the two of us began down the road to balancing chemical equations.

"Simone, there's a guy waving at you from back there." Pru and I arrived at Chemistry to find Seth flagging me to sit in the empty seat near him. It was a table of four and there was already Seth and the same Puerto Rican guy I remembered from Riot sitting across from him. They were both smiling when Pru and I walked over there. "Don't worry," I whispered to her. "These guys are okay. The one with the blue eyes is my best friend." Pru studied both of them shyly and I sat down next to Seth. He began to massage my hand and it made me feel all sorts of weird and tingly. I shivered before I realized that he didn't seem mad at me anymore. I wondered why...

"Sim, why don't you introduce us to your fine friend here." Seth said teasingly, smiling at Pru. I cleared my throat and said, "Okay, well, Seth this is Prudence. Prudence this is Seth."

They exchanged friendly smiles and she said. "Pru—just call me Pru."

"And this here is Tony." Seth declared, never taking his eyes off me. I bit my lip, nervous and sort of turned on by this outspoken side of my best friend. I ought to be smote for looking at him like that, but dang, I couldn't help it.

Tony extended his hand out to Pru and she shook it. "Pleasant meeting you, Pru." She smiled and averted her gaze to me. We both frowned at the behavior of the guys and I began to notice Tony's lingering gaze on my new friend. Apparently, Pru felt it because she used a slightly shaking hand to put her micro braids behind her ear. Tony licked his lips before saying to her, "How long have you known, uh, Simone?"

She looked startled that he spoke to her and she replied, "U-Um, well, we met a while ago." She nodded and added lamely, "How about you?" Tony looked at me then and I rolled my eyes. "We have mutual friends. Plus, I've seen her from around." That was true. I barely knew his name and only that because Seth was always hanging with him in my absence. I never really acknowledged his skater buddies because they never seemed that interested in me. So, I just minded my own business and usually that business was Seth Montgomery. The two continued a quiet conversation when the teacher came in and began to teach. Seth kept his large hand around mine and stroked my palm with his thumb. I couldn't focus on the lesson with him doing that and I didn't want my grade to fall, so I slipped from his grip and began to take notes. But he was persistent, and when I started writing his hand went to my thigh and slid higher to pull up my dress and—

I punched the shit out of him, straight to the wrist. I was aiming to hit his gut, but he was tall and my short arm could only reach so far. He retreated it quickly then and hissed, "Ah crap, Sim! That hurt, why'd you do that for?"

I glared daggers. "What the hell is wrong with you?"

Mr. King, the teacher, looked back at us and proclaimed, "Is there a problem back there? 'Cause if there is I can separate the two of you."

"No problem here, sir." I said. He went back to his lesson and I resumed my argument with the tall jerk beside me. "Well?"

A tic started in his jaw before he answered coldly, "I know there's someone else." I coughed when he said that because it took me so off guard. He knew about Jerome and the deal we had? How the hell was everyone learning personal information about me lately? Was I wearing my autobiography on my shirt or something? "What do you mean?" I demanded.

He ignored me and glared at the chalk board.

I punched him again on the hip and he said, "Shit, will you stop doing that? You punch like a freaking linebacker." Rubbing his sore spot he continued, "I know...there's another guy, and I'm not the jealous type, but..." My heartbeat slowed when I realized he knew nothing about Jerome and our deal. I sighed in relief. "Oh, um...it's not what you think." I said normally. "I'm not seeing anyone, you know that. I'm not that pretty."

Seth shook his head then said, "So, will you go with me to the movies today?" His tone was sarcastic, as if he was proving a point. I was angry now and so I retorted, "Seth, I already told you I can't!"

He pursed his lips and nodded, "All right. I got you." When class ended, Seth and Tony sped away, leaving Pru and I alone to watch after them practically make dust on the linoleum.

One o' clock. The dreaded and designated time I was supposed to meet Jerome at his house to carry out the "plan". Well, it was blackmail and I was unwilling to stop it so I decided to take it with dignity. Actually, my own plan was to sway him in another direction. You know, talk him out of it? Mostly because I thought I had at least a fighting chance of sweet talking myself out of this so I can dig up some dirt on him. Hey, if he could dig that deep into my life and retrieve all that information, then I figured I could do the same with him. I just needed a starting point. I didn't know where to start and get this, "top secret" information.

Holy crap was I stupid! Of course I knew where to start, and her name was Georgia. His sister of all people should know some sort of private information about that maniac. Now all I had to do was pick her up from school, even though that wasn't a part of the plan, and grill her.

I pulled onto the curb of 317 Fort Street and saw a guy on the porch, doing push-ups. He was in his own little zone when I honked my horn and called, "I can leave if you want! After all, I did cut school to be here and commit a sin and all..."

Jerome stood up then, and a slow smile spread across his handsome face. The bastard, why must he be so damn sexy? I mean, he was making this situation sort of easy, but I still had my values and that's what made me want to talk him out of it more than ever. When I got out of my car, I walked around it and met him midway on the porch steps. We just stood there for a while—me glaring and him smiling evilly. That expression made me want punch him and kiss him at the same time, but the anger was much stronger. So, taking that into account he uttered, "Ready?" and I punched him with as much force as I could exert, in his jaw. We wrestled for a time on the front porch until he had me pinned on the floor; my dress rode all the way up to my waist. He looked down at that, wiped the blood from his face, and smiled. I could see small splatters of blood in his teeth when I spat, "Fuck you!" My attempts for swaying and wooing him went out the window and all I wanted then was his blood. He laughed, stood up and lifted me in his arms to begin carrying me inside the house. "Isn't that why you're here?" He asked calmly as he ran up the steps and into a room down the hall. Once inside, he threw me—hard—onto the large bed and my vision blurred for a second. He began to take his clothes off and was down to his boxers in a flash. He started on those as well until he saw my face and frowned in concern. "Oh, boo don't cry. It'll be quick and you can leave at two, for real."

"What?" I screamed. That's when I felt my face heated and tears cascading. He sat next to me on the bed, pulled my dress up over my head, and threw it into the hamper by his closet door. I watched how he treated the dress like trash when I held it to the highest esteems. I felt hopeless then and I whispered brokenly, "Please don't do this...I'm so scared." I felt so vulnerable and he put both of his hands to his face to hide it. When he resurfaced he said, "All right, all right. Since I'm a nice guy, I'll shorten your sentence to three weeks, but that's as low as I'm going."

I turned away from him then, as he stripped me, slid the both of us inside the covers and painfully put an end to any sort of virtue, and dignity, I had.

Abandoned conscience

I couldn't let it happen

Wouldn't show my vulnerability

Stayed in the recess of my thoughts

In the shadows that hid the beauty I never saw

From love to loathe

From shame to worthlessness

I dared not emerge from

The despair within the CAVE

-Simone Randon

Chapter Ten

Conscience Abandoned

That weekend...

I considered killing myself—again. However, I knew I could have never carried through with that plan. Besides, when I tried that last time, I worried everyone to death, especially Seth. I knew he loved me too much, so I couldn't let go. Speaking of which, I remembered I indirectly promised him the movies and no matter how much like crap I felt, I knew I had to do it for my friend. Even though he was acting totally like a prick the other day, I still couldn't say no to him that easily.

Currently, I was in bed sulking. Sulking over so many things, but mostly over my losses and defeats. I let Jerome win and that's what was gnawing at me. I was a strong willed girl and was rarely known to back down like that. Seriously, I'm such a loser. A loser of my self-worth, self-love...and a lot of other things.

Attempting to distract my feelings of depletion, I rolled (literally) out of bed and trudged inside the kitchen feeling sore in unmentionable areas. I went to the refrigerator and my eyes watered at the delicious sight when I opened it.

Strawberry cheesecake—an entire tray, too!

I was sort of dieting since that day people allowed me to think too much and I nearly off'd myself. So now I was the black sheep in the family who needed supervision at certain times of the day. Well, I did have some sort of freedom now I was eighteen, but still. I still didn't trust myself sometimes when I had thoughts like that, and when I did, I found myself purposely engaged in some kind of activity. Such as listening to Black Eyed Peas songs. Ha, they're awesome. "Is someone here?" I called.

No answer.

Great, because I knew my mother would freak if she stomped downstairs to see me doing this to myself. Well, she didn't mind me eating, but when I *binged* she would have a fit. Huh, I always thought that was funny when someone referred to someone else as *binging*.

It was like sophisticatedly calling someone a fatty. Anyway, when it occurred to me that no one was home I began to tear through the cake. I had only one bite of the berried heaven until it came to an abrupt end when the phone rang. No—screamed. I bellowed out in rage—feeling like the on-call cowgirl—and stomped over toward the phone. Who the hell was calling here? On a Saturday afternoon, the slowest and laziest day of the week? It was a wonder why I even picked it up at all. When I reached the living room, or the red room, I picked it up and answered resigned, "Hello?"

"Sim?" Of course, Seth. "Are you okay? You sound depressed."

I snorted. "I'm feeling okay." I could hear a whining voice in the background and it was no wonder who that was. That little boy was the devil. "Cody, shut *up* already will ya'?"

"Hey, is that Simone, Seth?" He asked distantly, sounding a little hopped up on sugar.

Seth sighed in irritation and I could tell that he had his hand entwined in his little brother's hair from the little yelp through the phone. "Go away, Cody!"

"No!" He screamed. I actually had to distance the phone from my ear it was so piercing. Yes, puberty failed him. Right about then I could also tell that Seth had cupped Cody's face in his hands. "Cody, will you please go to your room until I'm finished my conversation?" His voice was gentle now, as if he were lulling someone to sleep.

"All right..." Cody muttered and his voice was gone. Seth sighed and said to me, "*Any-who*, I just called to say I was sorry about yesterday and to ask if you wanted to chill out today. I mean, I'm free if..."

I nodded vigorously. "Yes, I would like that very much. And you're forgiven."

"Oh, um, okay." I guess the compliance shocked him a bit. "So, what do you want to do today?"

I pursed my lips in thought. The movies still didn't seem like a bad idea, because I initially *wanted* to do that. "You don't want to go to the movies? Like you asked?"

There was a pause until, "Yes!"He sounded truly excited until he cleared his throat and said finally, "Seriously? Am I talking to the real Simone Randon? Because, normally, when I would ask you to do something you're-you're difficult. I just...are you sure? What time do you want me to pick you up?"

I laughed, feeling momentarily all right with him. "How about an hour from now? Like, one o' clock?"

"U-Uh, sure. I'll be there."

"Okay, see you then." I agreed and began to hang up when I suddenly heard Seth say, "Oh, and Sim?"

I frowned, "Huh?"

I could hear the smile behind his words when he said, "I believe in you babe."

For the first time in a long time, I really appreciated the words, especially when I didn't believe in myself. Smiling and choking back tears I said, "You're the best, Seth." After we said our final goodbyes, I walked over to where the cheesecake was setting on the countertop. Feeling slightly okay, I did something I never thought I could do on my own: I put it back in the refrigerator, not quite hungry anymore.

After a considerable amount of watching TV, I turned it off and went on up to my room. I hadn't left the living room since the call from Seth, because I just didn't feel like being cooped up any longer. I mean, I was sulking in that room for hours with the door locked, my parents hollering at me to clean it up, and eating myself into an early grave. I didn't think it was only that call that lifted my spirits, but the meaning behind everything. He called because he wanted to be around me when I didn't even want to be around me. I hated myself now, and he still wanted to be my friend. I would say I felt lucky, but lucky wasn't it.

Blessed was more like it—to have Seth in my life.

I could feel the tears falling then. I had no idea why, but it was just an emotion overload and I felt bombarded with sensations. I was just confused why he still liked me when I loathed myself so much I couldn't stand it. I was sniffling when I glanced over at my alarm clock to see that a half hour passed already. Seth would arrive soon, and I decided to get my wallowing ass in the shower. When I stripped down and tossed my nightgown in the hamper I was assailed with a turbulent reminder of yesterday. Jerome and how he hurt me and harshly treated my possessions. How he used me so easily because I was determined to protect my father. And I didn't forget that I had to later interrogate Georgia. Once I gained some juicy info I could take it to the police and he could go to jail. I would say that he could be arrested for assaulting a minor, but I was eighteen and he was twenty one (which Georgia randomly told me one day): two adults. And I could testify rape, but it was consensual and legal under the law's eyes.

More tears came, and I angrily swiped them away and hopped in the shower. The cold water felt refreshing and mixed in with my tears. Those tears of contentment gone, and traded with a sorrowful weep. I was sobbing softly now, and after a time I got out and dried myself. With the towel wrapped around my body, I sat at my desk and began to blow dry my hair. I couldn't hear it, but from my bed my cell lit up letting me know someone was calling. I'm telling you, everyone just loved to call me for some reason. I rolled my eyes; sure it was Seth and was thrown off when I went over to study the screen. I shut my eyes tightly when I saw the text—determined not to shed anymore tears. I was going to beat him somehow; I just had a lot of searching to do.

> **JEROME**: All right, I'm in the mood now. Hurry up nd come ova b4 my parentz & Georgia get bck 4rom shoppin.

"No!" I screamed at the phone, knowing he couldn't hear me. How could he do this? I know I unwillingly agreed to meet him at his beck and call, but still. I glanced at the clock and was torn over what to do. Seth would be here in, like, twenty minutes and I still had to put my clothes on and think about what to do. Short on time, I decided to let my hair remain curly and threw some black jeans on and a light sweater.

Once I was dressed I stood in the center of my room, my gaze alternating between the phone and the clock. Jerome or Seth. I thought of how Jerome made me feel—like crap. When I saw him, Georgia, or even thought of his name I would get instantly depressed. The dude knew just how to put a frown on my face and give me dangerous thoughts.

And then I thought of Seth. An automatic smile came to my lips and my heart did laps. My stomach felt like butterflies and I had an unbearable urge to embrace him in my arms. I loved how he loved me and showed me just how to like me. I still didn't like me, but at least I felt not so worthless when I was around him. That dude was the best antidepressant.

My eyes lingered on the clock and suddenly my decision was made. I turned my phone off and jammed it in my pocket before I marched eagerly down the steps and toward the strident car horn outside beckoning me for a somewhat fun filled afternoon.

Screw Jerome.

Chapter Eleven

USING SIGN LANGUAGE WITH THE BLIND

I couldn't breathe, I couldn't take it. The pressure and exertion was destroying me. "Ah!" Seth howled in laughter. We were watching the new movie *Cast Iron* starring plenty of British people I didn't know the names of. It was a comedy that had the two of us laughing so hard we were escorted to the back. It was dark inside and the most I could see was the movie and just a faint trace of people's faces. Not that I wanted to look at their face, but it was still really dark. I wasn't afraid of the dark, but it did give me a lot of time to think which was never any good. However, Seth and the movie didn't allow me much time to think, only laugh and enjoy this time with him. When someone said something funny, he'd repeat it in a weird way that would have me guffawing so hard I'd believe my ears would bleed.

"Whew!" I exhaled when the scene changed from the main character being beaten up by a horse to his wife chewing him out for instigating it. It was a pretty slow scene that left an opening for conversation. Finally, Seth turned and looked down at me for a time and then said, "Having a good time?"

I wiped my eyes from the tears of laughter and nodded. "Yes!"

He chuckled and reached over to massage my hand. It was just his way of feeling comfortable, I knew, and that involved touching things. Still, it reminded me of the way he tried to feel me up in Chemistry and I flinched a little. His hand retracted and he muttered, "Oh, sorry." He scratched his hair and when he met my eyes, his was twinkling from the light of the movie. It was such an affectionate expression that I found myself grabbing his hand in mine and holding it more tightly. Seth's blue eyes looked like flaming water and I smiled and said, "It's okay." He looked at me more intently and I said, "This is the best I've felt in days, and it's because of you. You're the best friend a girl could ever have." I gave his hand one final squeeze before whispering finally, "Thank you..."

Seth literally looked like he imploded.

He ran his hand through my curls and said softly, "I love your hair like this..." I smiled in appreciation before he gently clenched his hands in my hair and leaned down to kiss me. My arms did their best to wound around him, but in the end they were too short, so I settled for laying them gently on his chest. He moaned and wrapped his arms around me and brought me closer to him. Damn, he felt good. His roughness against my smoothness worked and made me deepen the kiss. This was what heaven must feel like, I thought as he began to massage my back. This dude must have had formal training in seducing a girl, because what he was doing had me craving him in a way I never really did before. We had our first kiss when we were seven, and it was after school when we were waiting for our moms to pick us up. I remembered after that he pulled back from me with the goofiest smile on his face saying, "You're my girl now." We giggled afterward and then my mother came to take me home. Funny how I remembered that day clearly and I was having recent problems remembering the quadratic formula.

But this kiss was nothing like our first one.

From behind us, I heard someone mutter, "Get a damn room," but I ignored it and continued the moment of bliss. My heart was beating fast and my adrenaline was pumping and sooner than I knew it I was unbuttoning Seth's fly. He growled and then his hands were on mine, halting me from pulling his pants down. "Simone, no, we can't do this now." His voice sounded tortured from restraint and that only egged me on. I moved his hands from mine and continued on. "But Seth..." My voice was a sensual caress and he moaned again before he shook his head, "N-No. I won't do this to you. Not now..." He zipped his pants back up and the applause from around us scared the shit out of me and brought me back down from cloud seventy. Looking up, I saw that the movie was over and realized that we'd been making out through the entire second half of it. All around us we heard, "Man that was funny!" "Did you *see* that ending?" "I want to watch that again!" "I feel sorry for anybody who missed *that* ending!"

I rolled my eyes and cleared my throat. I could feel that I was blushing, but when the two of us emerged from the movie room it was obvious that Seth was flushed as well. His cheeks were rosy and he was breathing all hard and his eyes were scanning the crowded lobby nervously. I composed myself and started for the door, Seth following. When we reached the outside we spotted his mother's truck he was using in the parking lot. There was a heavy silence between us as we walked quickly to the car. When we got there, Seth got in and unlocked my door. When I got in we just sat there, afraid to look at each other. I turned around first, and gazed lovingly at him. When he turned to look at me his expression was one of irritation. Now that made me frown and a little irritated too. "What?" I asked. He flailed his hands in the air and smacked them against the steering wheel. "You!" He shook his head and added, "When you look at me like that it makes me want to take advantage of you in the back of this car."

I smiled and said softly, my voice still an alluring whisper, "Take advantage of me, eh?"

"Ah!" He roared in frustration and leaned over to kiss me fiercely. I relished in the feel of his lips against mine and found myself shaking in restraint, trying extremely hard not to take his clothes off. He pulled back from me like he could sense my pain and closed his eyes, taking in deep breaths. Seth took one last mouthful of air and said, "Okay. I'm all right now."

I tried the voice again, "Oh really?"

He turned to me when the car was started and said, "Oh yeah. You're my girl now." I smiled at the memories he evoked with those words and had to force the tears back. God how I loved this guy...

"Thanks for the wonderful afternoon out." I said to Seth once he pulled up in front of my house. It was three-thirty and I knew my parents would be home around five-ish. I was out of the car, standing outside the window talking to him. "You're very welcome, my dear." He said, mimicking the weird accent of the guy in the movie we'd just seen. I threw my head back and laughed out loud. It was hilarious shit. We joked around for a bit more and later on in the conversation I decided to call it quits. I smiled one last time at him, said goodbye, and walked up to my porch steps. Seth pulled off and was driving down the road when I was fiddling with the lock on the door. My key was acting funny and once I miraculously got inside I saw, ironically, the shock of my life.

There, sitting on my red room couch, was Jerome Cooper.

I screamed.

Chapter Twelve

THE CAVE OF BLISS

"What the hell are you doing in here?" I shrieked. I was standing against the shut door behind me, pondering if I should run or not. I gulped and continued, "I'm calling the cops."

He chuckled and stood up. "Didn't you get my last twenty text messages, girl?" My eyes widened at how...hungry and deprived he looked. Even though he's normally crazy he usually owns this calmness that was sort of creepy. But now he just looked like he needed a V8 or something. "Didn't you!" He demanded, and I shuddered from the harshness of his tone. I unclenched my fists and felt around in my pocket for my phone.

It was gone.

Shit! I must have dropped it at the movie theater, or at the very worst, left it in Seth's car. I was screwed, and I couldn't really run across the room to call the cops because he would tell my father's secret and plus, he was way bigger than me! So I calmed myself and spoke to him in the same manner. "Jerome, listen. I didn't get your texts because I—I lost my phone, okay?"

He approached me then and grabbed my arm. "Whatever." He growled as he dragged me toward the couch. He began to tear away my sweater, and jeans and while doing that he said, "Oh, and by the way, I saw you're little boyfriend. I just want you to know that I could care less. Besides..." He smiled maniacally. "You gave *me* the honor of popping your cherry." He snorted. "Shows how much you love him, huh?"

Now that seriously pissed me off. How could he just come into my house and talk to me like that? "You *asshole!*" I shouted and started raining punches on his chest and face. He pinned my arms down and squeezed my wrists till I thought my veins would burst. The pain brought tears to my eyes and I sobbed, "Stop...just leave me alone already. Haven't I suffered enough?"

When I was completely naked, and he from the waist down, he frowned and said sardonically, "That's the fun in this, boo." And without a moment's hesitation he violated me and the happiness I felt before was out the window. With every pant, I was reminded of how much I hated myself and how much I wanted to die. Seriously, I wish he'd just freaking kill me already so that I wouldn't have to go through with the mental and physical torture. "*Mmm!*" He moaned. I cringed and cried harder and louder and things were moving faster and I felt a little dizzy and—

I heard the door open.

"Sim? Is that you?" He paused. "What the fuck?" Jerome stopped instantly and turned towards a crazy-eyed Seth. I was sobbing so loudly I could barely form words to explain. "You left your phone in the car...oh *fuck* this!" I expected him to abandon me. After all, who would want to stay by my side and not see me for the trash I was. My vision was blurred and when I blinked the tears away I saw that Seth hadn't left me and that he was fighting a half assed naked Jerome in my red room. Currently, I was lying on the couch with my legs propped open and exposed. Shrieking in rage I jumped up and involved myself in the fight. From another perspective I probably looked like the frisky little midget that tried to fight off the evil giants or something. I hissed when Jerome's fist missed Seth and struck me instead. The force was so juggernaut, I found myself on the floor and crawling toward the kitchen. My jaw was so sore and I could feel the blood coursing down my chin. "DON'T YOU EVER HIT SIMONE—YOU SORRY FUCK!" I heard Seth threaten loudly from the red room, and then more grunts and powerful punches to the flesh. I was groaning in pain, standing still for a moment and just holding my face. It felt as if it were throbbing. I was hearing yells and I had a feeling it was Seth getting hurt. I would be damned if I allowed that bastard to hurt Seth. No, it was not going down like that.

I looked up then and spotted my mother's expensive catalogued knives. Whimpering, I dashed for the sharpest one and grabbed it. When the weapon was in my hands I closed my eyes and did something I hadn't done in years.

I prayed.

I stopped praying because I used to think that God punished me by making me fat. I realized now that it was my own fault and that I needed him now more than ever. Once finished, I walked slowly into the red room and opened my eyes. The two guys were still fighting hard, and there was a lot of blood being shed on the red carpet. When Jerome had Seth on the ground he stood and kicked him squarely in the head.

That was when I lost it.

Screaming, I dashed for Jerome when his back was turned and the knife ran smoothly in his side. He screeched, turned around, back handed me, and finally we both fell to the floor, defeated. I wasn't unconscious like he was, but everyone was on the floor. I once again crawled weakly (still naked) over to where Seth dropped my phone and grabbed it. My hands were shaking when I tried to dial 9-1-1, but I somehow managed. The operator answered and I blubbered, "Please, somebody come help!"

The last thing I remembered was giving the operator my address before passing out.

Chapter Thirteen

Drinking Dry Ice

"I see I'm gonna' have to get the law on that little punk's ass again...he just loves to tempt me." I heard a deep voice say from...somewhere around me. Currently, there was darkness, and all I was aware of was the out-of-body feeling and the voices. I would say I was in pain, because I usually was, but I would have been lying. Right then, I felt that numb-like floating-on-a-cloud feeling—which wasn't feeling at all.

"Don't go easy on him this time." A feminine, but firm, voice demanded. The other voice chuckled darkly and said, "Oh, if I gave you those thoughts then I'm sorry to mistake you. His ass is grass, I'm serious, and I'm talking jail time." Whoever these people were they were mad. I mean, I could practically taste the resentment in the air. After a considerable amount of shuffling there was another voice that broke in that made me ponder my situation.

"OH MY GOSH! Simone, please be okay!" My eyes fluttered open to reveal a tear jerked Luz hovering over me. I could see now, and looking around I saw that my parents were there and so was my crazy cousin. Wait a minute...how could this be right? She was supposed to be in New York, and even if she was going to visit it would have taken her about two days to get here. Well damn, she could've warned me. "L-Luz?" I said thickly, "Is that you?"

She gasped, "Oh my gosh! Aunt Ashleigh I think she woke up!" The feminine voice was full of emotion when she answered, "Yes, Luz—we see that." It was later when I realized that those voices I heard previously were my parents, Zachary and Ashleigh. Huh, maybe I was dreaming when I heard them say...

"Simone? Honey are you okay?" I heard my father ask. I could feel the thickness in my speech and noticed that there were probably gauzes in my mouth. I had to compose myself and adjust the thick padding in my jaw. I nodded, "Yeah."

My eyes were in slits and I could barely make out the tall figure of Zachary Randon. When he approached me, he laid a gentle hand on my shoulder. "Everything's gonna be okay now, baby—I'll be sure of that." His face was red when added, "I didn't go that hard on the little bastard because it would've made you unhappy. But now, it's an entirely different ball game."

"Thanks dad," I whispered.

"Someone has to go." My mother's voice said. I looked over at her—her face was red too and I could tell she'd been crying. She continued, "The doctor said only two people at a time can be here." My parents looked pointedly at Luz.

She frowned back at them. "If y'all think I'm leaving, then don't hold your breath. I had to sneak passed the nurses to get here!" They only looked at her, seemingly more irritated. "I. Ain't. Goin." She said and began waving at them. "One of y'all better get the heck out of here."

"All right." My father said sharply. He kissed me on the forehead, grabbed my mother's hand and the two of them walked out. Yeah, Luz and my dad never really got along. They were very competitive and always challenging each other, but this time I guess his patience ran out.

Luz approached me the second my parents shut the door and said, "Oh my gosh—tell me *everything* that happened." I sighed and gargled down the saliva that was accumulating in my mouth. She seemed to understand how much of a difficulty it would've been for me to speak and said, "Oh! I'm sorry I forgot about that...so, you wanna' write it down?"

"Luz!" I blubbered. My jaw was hurting now.

She put her hands up in surrender. "Sorry! I just didn't come all this way to sit in silence. I do that enough at home."

I frowned at that. "But you have twin sisters!"

She nodded and gave me a 'duh' look. "Uh-huh, but Lolita and Liana are juniors in college and I'm a new senior in high school. So, I have some personal experience with silence."

I sighed and whispered slowly, "What do you want to know?"

Luz began to squirm in anticipation. "Um, okay, who is this guy that raped you?"

I tried to grind my teeth, but the gauzes prevented it. Now that question made me feel like shit all over again and the memories rushed me. I remembered the phone call with the police and Jerome breaking into my house and Seth getting hurt—

"Seth!" I said loudly, which hurt my jaw even more. I jerked upright in the hospital bed and swung my legs over it. I had to get to him! Luz's hands were steadying me. "Wait a minute *chica* you've got to rest.

Lay back down." The hospital dress I had on covered nothing, but I did not care. I needed to know if Seth was okay, and lying around wasn't helping anything. I inched towards the door and she blocked it. "Luz, move! I need to see him!"

She scowled. "The dude that raped you?"

I shook my head and pushed her aside. "No! I need to see if Seth is all right...*mmh*." I groaned from the pain talking had caused me. Damn that Jerome! The next time I saw him, I was going to hit his ass in the jaw. Luz's expression went from irritated to sad. What the hell was wrong with her? "Simone...sit down. I need to tell you something."

My eyes widened. "No!" I whispered, tears in my eyes. I wouldn't believe it, I couldn't. There was no way I was going to believe that my best friend in the whole world was—

"Simone, the guy you're talking about then, the other one in the fight, he's...in surgery." She looked down, averting her gaze. I saw a tear slip down her face when she finished, "I didn't want to tell you, because I wasn't sure if Seth was the one who raped you or not. But if you're talking about him, then I overheard the doctors saying that there's no real hope for him. Said his head was hit so forcibly that it affected his brain...or something...I'm so sorry Mo."

"*What?*" I shrieked. "Seth is fine...he's fine..." I chanted over and over. It felt as if my every move was causing me more debilitating pain. I was cradling my jaw while maneuvering my cousin from the front door. Unfortunately, she was a stubborn wench and refused to move away. The pain eventually got the best of me and she was dragging me back to my bed. She laid me carefully back down and was recovering me while saying, "You'll have to talk to the doctor, Mo. I-I'm not all that sure..."

"Seth is fine...Seth is fine...Seth is fine..." I was shaking my head back and forth, and reciting that over and over. It would be fair to say that I was in shock. Basically, it was because there was no way I believed the fact that my *best* friend was dead. No, because if that happened, then I don't know if I could ever live with myself. How I could wake up every morning with any sort of self love or self-esteem. My...best friend better be okay. "Simone, girly, it's okay! I'm sorry if I upset you, um, I'll go get Aunt Ashleigh if—"

"Momo?" A soft voice with an accent called from the door. I wasn't paying any attention—I just wanted Seth. I needed him right then; he was my comfort, my joy, my...rock. I didn't know what I would've done with myself if he was dead. I truly didn't. Luz was immediately on her guard. "Uh—excuse me—who are you?"

Georgia came closer and countered, "Well I'm here to see my *friend!*" She snarled. I would've been amazed had I not been so damn worried for Seth's well being. Georgia came up to me and frowned, "Are you okay?"

"Simone, who the hell is she?" Luz asked, disconcerted.

I was trembling when I shouted, "SETH!"

Both girls were hovering over my bed and massaging my shoulders. "Don't cry, don't cry, I'm here..." Someone was saying but I wasn't listening. I was rocking now, looking like a crazy person, and both girls were holding me. "Seth..." I whimpered. I just felt so out of place. Without Seth here I didn't even want to like myself. He was my motivator.

I didn't know when things quieted down, but they did. There was panting and Luz and Georgia was looking at me, worry etched in their features. I looked at them helplessly and felt the tears fall. My jaw still hurt like hell when Georgia said gravely, "Jerome's going to jail."

Now that I paid attention to. I sniffled, "Really?"

She nodded and answered, "Yeah."

"Is that who raped you?" Luz asked, confused.

"Yeah." Georgia said, not meeting her gaze.

"And what about Seth?" I asked frantically.

Georgia just looked away.

I had to face the fact that Seth was dead. I didn't know how I would—or if I could—do it. Seth was my motivator, my everything. I wasn't sure if I could go on in life without him, but I was sure of one thing: I would soon have to. I knew if I were to kill myself it would hurt Seth, alive or dead. And I was never one to intentionally harm anyone, especially Seth. I loved him...

I love him.

That's when Luz lost it. "Listen chick, if you don't tell her what's wrong with him then I'll shove my foot so far up your—"

"Luz, stop it." I said quietly, drowning in my emotions. I could not handle controlling someone else right then...I was too fragile myself. I placed a hand on her clenched fists (she was ready to swing) and added, "Let her explain."

"All right." Luz composed herself and folded her arms across her chest. "Explain." She demanded of Georgia.

Georgia looked nervous, but complied anyway in the end. "Seth...he's not dead."

My eyes widened. "REALLY?" I asked with *way* more feeling. More hope. I needed for him to be okay for me to be okay. Georgia shook her head, "But he's not okay."

"What do you mean?" Luz asked eagerly (her fists poised).

Georgia took a deep breath. "Jerome shattered two of his ribs and nearly got his heart, so the doctor told us. He kicked his head too—narrowly missing his temple." She looked away again. "H-He was dead when he arrived at the hospital a few hours ago, but they revived him." I saw a tear slip down her cheek. "I'm so sorry Jerome did this, I didn't think it would get this far—"

"Seth...is alive?" I rasped. I didn't care nor did I want Jerome's sob story. I wanted Seth; it was as simple as that.

She met my gaze steadily when she said, "For now, yes. But..."

"Girl—" Luz almost pounced on her, but I was quick to block her.

"Luz, sit still before I punch the living *shit* outta' you!" I growled. She grounded her teeth and was eerily still. I looked at Georgia to allow her to continue and she did. "Tell me about Seth!" I gargled. Darn my stupid jaw.

She sighed and wiped the tears from her eyes. "He's in a coma."

She barely finished her sentence when I started for the door.

Chapter Fourteen

Outstretched Arms

"Miss Randon, you shouldn't be out of bed." I heard a *stern voice say. I didn't turn* around to see who it was because I didn't care. I just cared for where I was going next and that place was pretty clear.

I stopped in the center of the hallway and turned to face Luz, Georgia, and the nurse I supposed was trying to appease me. She opened her mouth to say something else, but I raised a hand to stop her. "Where is Jerome Cooper's room?" I asked steadily, careful not to afflict any more pain to my jaw.

She frowned. "Is this a family member, or—"

Damn, I forgot about that. You couldn't visit someone without them being a blood relative. Now I had to make up something that would get me to that bastard—

"Y-Yes." Georgia piped up. "He's actually my brother and..." She stopped to think and the nurse began to look skeptic.

"You see, we're all cousins." Luz motioned around the group, indicating the three of us. I opened my mouth to refute that but thought better of it. If this was my only way of getting to him, then so be it—I guess I was his cousin now. Luz fidgeted and added, "See the resemblance?" The nurse studied us all and I think we had her. It was only coincidental that all three of us owned tanned skin. I was still thinking of the irony of the situation while I watched the nurse debate with herself. She sighed in defeat and studied a paper she had in her hands. "You said Cooper, right?"

I nodded vigorously, "Yes, ma'am."

She looked tired when she said, "All right, I'll show you where his room is, but only two of you can go in there. I'm giving you ten minutes. That's it."

She led us to one of the many rooms down the hall and finally stopped in front of the door. She kept her back to the door while she warned, "I'm warning you—only ten minutes." She looked to me and held my gaze. Her features softened a degree. "I can lose my job if my boss finds out."

"We understand!" We all said, weirdly, in unison.

The nurse scanned the perimeter and paced quickly down the hall. When she was completely gone, I gulped once for strength and said, "I'm going in alone." I turned to both of their frowns and said finally, "This isn't a party—it's a confrontation. Now I need you guys to wait out here and knock on the door if I'm in there for ten minutes or more. Okay?"

Georgia nodded eagerly, "Gotcha."

I turned to Luz, she was pouting. "Luz?" I asked.

She rolled her eyes and said tiredly, "Fine. I got you."

"Thanks guys." I inhaled deeply and pushed the door open to a series of calm beeps. I shut the door behind me and turned to the silent monster a few feet away from me. He was laying dissonantly still and I was scared as hell to move an inch. I seemingly forgot the tiny fact that he was my biggest fear at that point. Just the very sight of him was enough to piss me off and have me running like there was no tomorrow. I heard my heartbeat accelerate and I knew my nerves had betrayed me. Know what, why was I here in the first place? Totally chickening out, I turned around and placed my hand on the knob to have my conscience scream at me to be brave. *Come on Sim,* I could hear Seth's deep voice whisper in my mind. *I believe in you babe.* Okay, now that definitely helped get me together. I clenched my fists, put on my best war face, and marched right up to Jerome. "Wake up you bastard!" I hissed when I neared him. I waited for about two minutes, and when I saw that he was still sleeping it only heightened my fury to immeasurable lengths. *"Wake up!"* I screeched and I hadn't realized my hands were balled into tight fists and nearing his face until his eyes opened sluggishly. They were distant for a minute before he turned and his eyes focused on me. His eyes were pinkish and I frowned in concern. "Simone...is that you?" He rasped, exhausted. I only gawked at him while he smiled pleasantly and whispered, "*Sweet* Simone...where you at?"

It felt as if the air was thickening and I stuttered. "Um...yeah. I-It's me..."

He smiled. "Good. Because I'm gonna kick your ass when I get the chance." He said this so lazily and drowsily that I almost forgot that it was a threat. I gulped and glanced down at the bandaging around his entire abdominal area. Where I stabbed him...

Guilt rushed me and I realized just how low I was stooping. I came here to kick a wounded man when he was down, and that was a punk move. That was a non-Simone-like move. I knew Seth wouldn't condone something like this and I also knew that I was becoming the very thing that my father threw in jail: a coward. So I lowered my hand and backed away from him, forever, I never wanted to see him again. Sadly, even if that meant ridding Georgia from my life as well. She was annoying, but she sort of grew on me.

Too bad I'd have to let her go.

He was laughing softly with his eyes closed when I reached the door. I would have cried, but what he did to me, to Seth, made him undeserving of my tears. I shook my head, shut my eyes, and pushed the door open. "Simone, you all right?" I heard Luz asked. When I opened my eyes I saw Georgia and Luz watching me like deer caught in the headlights. I was gazing up into their eyes when I answered, "I will be."

"I know where Seth's room is, you know?" Georgia said distantly. I smiled, not even mad at her for omitting this information, and said, "Good. Take me there."

***

True tears were coursing down my face at the sight.

We'd found the same nurse who let us inside Jerome's room and we goaded her into allowing me inside Seth's room. He was in intensive care and currently I was inside his room, looking at the wires and machines hooked up to him, weeping. It was such a spontaneous thing, how I ended up in his room. I wanted to smile at the easiness of it all until I came back to reality and zeroed in on my best friend's face. There were scars on his forehead and he was pale. It was a direct contrast, and it made his hair appear pitch black. Ignoring the pain in my jaw I wiped the tears from my face and lied, "You look great, you know?" He didn't answer of course, but talking to him distracted me from thinking too much and getting in even more trouble than I was already in. I sniffed and replied anyway, "Yeah, you always were a looker, huh?"

Silence. This time it killed me and I broke down. I just felt so guilty that I couldn't bottle it up any longer. The high hospital bed reached up to about my breast area and I wanted to keel over and apologize, but realized that I'd only be under the bed and solving nothing. So I remained upright and decided to pour my heart out to Seth, the guy I loved to pieces. Looking around, I grabbed a chair and slid it over to his side. For a while I just sat there and gazed at him. Thinking of all the good times and the bad times and the ugly times. I thought of how he made me feel when...I even thought about him. I didn't have to be near him to feel his love and that's why I loved him the way I did. He was my rock and I'd wanted would fight for him—I'd believe in him, because that's what he'd do for me, and I knew it. Taking a deep breath, I closed my eyes and began, "About four years ago, as you know, my family went into debt and was forced to declare bankruptcy." I choked on a sob partly because it felt good to say it out loud and that I felt like I was betraying my dad. "...a-and one day this guy calls my dad and tells him about this case. It was a civil dispute within this family, the Shay family, and the guy promised that my dad would make a lot of money if he won the case. However, he was supposed to defend Mr. Heath Shay who claimed he saw his wife, Liz, using drugs in front of their two-year-old daughter, Jenna. Well...Liz was a former drug addict and my dad, unfortunately, had to win the case in the favor of Mr. Shay.

"He turned the offer down at first, but he later realized that he had to do it, because we were, you know, *really* broke and the house was being foreclosed. Remember the slumber parties we used to have?" I paused for a minute, remembering how that was the longest period I ever stayed away from home. We were about fourteen, and I could still recall those long nights we'd stay up with his mom Ms. Montgomery (I know, we were dorks) watching Star Wars. I smiled inwardly, stealing myself a moment of bliss before having to continue. "I'm only telling you this because you're the only one I trust with something this...exclusive. And I—before I chicken out—want to tell you that I love you Seth." I was crying hard now and was so glad that no one could see me. The only one I ever let see me cry was...well damn, Seth.

I held my jaw in my hands and continued on with my story, "Later on, the court was noticing that Liz was innocent, so she was pretty much winning. My dad was happy for her, really, but...if he didn't win that case there would be no money coming and we would have been on the streets. Well, Liz pretty much had the court on her side until, um..." I was blubbering and shaking my head. I looked at Seth's unmoving body and steady breathing and asked, "Do you really want to hear what happened?"

He took a deep breath and I took that as a green light. I inhaled and said, "...before the case could be over and done with...they had to perform a drug test to make sure there was no drugs in her body and...my dad got desperate." I closed my eyes tightly and said hurriedly, "My dad spiked the drug test to make it look like she was using when she wasn't." I could feel my face heating from my nerves and was choking on my sobs. I cried a long time because it felt good to let the demons go. It felt good to just let go and *talk* about it. For a long time I just sat there and cried it out. Determined to finish it, I sniffled and said, "Liz lost the case, her daughter, and went to jail. My dad won and was paid a butt load of money. Things were looking up for us until the week following the case. Mr. Shay gained custody of their daughter and...he ended up..." I could barely get the words out. "That week, the police discovered the bodies of Mr. Shay and his daughter Jenna dead in the family household. He committed suicide and left a note that said he felt unworthy to live and that his daughter had to die too, because h-he didn't want to go alone..." I had no idea why, but I watched him with the belief that he'd sit up, reach down and hug me. I needed to feel him with me somehow, and right now I knew if I didn't leave then I'd end up tackling him. And I had a feeling that he, nor his mother, would appreciate that.

Ever so gently, I leaned down and placed the lightest kiss upon his forehead. When I stood back to view him I noticed the tears stains I left on his forehead and gently wiped them away. "I love you, Seth." I whispered before I opened the door and walked out.

Chapter Fifteen

MAY OCTOBER NOVEMBER END

Things may have seemed like they were moving fast in the beginning, but were nothing compared to now. A week had passed since I'd been released from the hospital and I was, of course, in my room. I tried to make it a point to visit Seth every day, but my own injuries hindered from doing so. My jaw was not as bad as it was last week, but it still bothered me to speak some. However, the pain was an awesome excuse from school for a week, and I was always gung-ho for something like that.

As I established, I was in my room and not watching TV for once. My mother had said she thought I was addicted to *Lifetime*, and I agreed with her. So I decided to change, and that enabled me to do something productive with my leisure.

Like actually clean my room.

I was in my Oliver Twist clothes and scrubbing and dusting every crevice and contour of my room. It would be fair to say that I was doing this to take my mind off the terrible image of Seth lying on the hospital bed, vulnerable. I came to terms though and accepted the obvious and inevitable. The chances of Seth coming back were slim and as much as it gnawed at me I forced myself to tolerate his absence. I had to be strong for him and for me.

It was easier that way to move on.

I cleared the sweat from my forehead and decided to tackle the mess of a backpack that was lying haphazardly on the floor. Everything else was pretty much clean, except the eyesore of a backpack glaring at me. My joints were kinked and my muscles ached and all I wanted was a hot shower and a good *Lifetime* movie.

Sighing, I trudged over to the bag and began sorting through the many papers I randomly threw inside it. I found my Chemistry homework I never turned in and already was devising an excuse for it, until a folded piece of paper fell out and landed on the floor beside my backpack. I frowned, its smallness attracting me, and kicked the bag away. What was written on the front made me feel like shit. "Crap!" I hissed when I read Pru's writing indicating her phone number inside. Good going Simone, I told myself, you finally make a friend and totally forget about her existence altogether. I huffed and fell backwards on my bed—mussing my sheets. I couldn't just ignore the fact that she asked me to dinner, because I promised her and I was never one to back down on a promise.

Standing up, I dusted my raggedy clothes off and started for my bathroom (a built-in bathroom, talk about convenient for a time like now). When I stripped, I hopped in the shower and set the water temperature to high. The heat scalded me and I gave a little yelp, but didn't change it. It felt good.

When I finished bathing, I opened the door to my room—a steam fog following me on my way out. Now that was rejuvenating! It didn't only cleanse me physically, but it helped get my head together. I was focusing so hard on the cons of Seth's absence that I did not even notice the simple things like my friend's dinner invitation. Heck, I was so deep in thought I hadn't noticed *anything*, especially the figure sitting on my bed when I walked out of the bathroom...naked. Now seeing that brought back some terrible memories and made me scream.

"Calm down Simone!" My mother's voice penetrated the steamy haze that formed in my room. "It's not like I've never seen you naked before."

I snatched a towel from the rail on my bathroom wall and wrapped myself with it. Jeez! She knew I was a prude. I placed a hand to my racing heart and said hurriedly, "Oh my goodness—mom—you nearly sent me into cardiac arrest!"

She shook her head and rolled her eyes. "Such a drama queen. It's only a wonder where you got that from."

I huffed, proving her right, and said, "What are you doing here?"

She looked offended, "Why, last I checked, I lived here." She laughed at my smirk and said, "Okay, seriously, I just came in here to talk to you. Are you all right?" Her features softened and I instantly knew what she meant. Of course, how could I forget about, "the talk"? Many thought I'd been raped when I actually wasn't. It was an agreement Jerome, but mostly him, and I came to to keep my father from going to prison.

I clenched the towel tighter and nodded, "Y-Yeah, I'm good."

"Are you sure? Because I didn't come here to pressure you or anything." I gritted my teeth together to keep from bawling. I really didn't want to talk about that subject right then. The wounds he inflicted were just too raw right now—it still hurt to talk about it...literally. So I lied, "Yeah, I'm sure mom." She was actually making me nervous with the subject.

She looked as if she was going through some sort of internal conflict, but she settled on saying, "Uh...just be sure...you know about the dangers and risks of sex, right? We've talked about STD's and teenage pregnancy and stuff..."

I had no idea why, but she angered me with this and the next thing I knew my stupid ass blurted, "Mom, he used protection every time..."

Her eyes widened at that and she said, "Oh, so you've done it before?"

I felt my cheeks redden and I took a few cautious steps back, afraid she would just start swinging or something.

I expected fury—come on, after all she was a Rodriguez at heart— but instead she looked deeply sad. Her eyes were glassy and I knew what else was coming. Shaking her head, my mother put her head in her hands and began to cry. "I swear Simone, you make me feel like a failure when you...oh!" Her crying became noisy and she continued to blubber, "When you continue to do these things—starve yourself, cut yourself, get in fights, have *sex!*—you make me, your dad too, feel like a failure as a parent."

I could feel the tears prick my eyes, too, because she was making me feel bad. When she listed my past and current faults it reopened old wounds and I felt hurt. I couldn't stand it when, every time I'd try to feel less ashamed, people would still manage to get me down. Everyone, I could tell, hated me. And I was so tired of making people hate me, tired of me hating me, that I was determined not to convert my own parents.

I approached my mother and sat next to her on my bed. I placed a hand on her shoulder and said, "I know mom, and I'm sorry. I really am."

She came from the concealment of her hands and said stuffily, "Sweetheart, I don't need an apology. I just want you to be happy, and I don't like what I'm seeing. Honey, stop feeling sad for everybody. You take everyone's problems and worry yourself to tears over them." She smiled. "That face we gave you is too pretty to have a frown on it."

I chuckled at that and said, "Thanks mommy."

She grinned and opened her arms. I hugged her and it felt good. There was no anger, sadness, or stress, just a loving gesture. A hug was what I needed and I found myself wanting her to know everything. I wanted to let go and share my worries with someone else, like my mother advised me. I could feel a tear slip down my cheek when I whispered, "He threatened me, mom. That's why I did it..."

She pulled back and said, alerted, "Who? When? What?"

I looked away and continued, "J-Jerome. He made me have sex with him mom—it wasn't rape, but he still *made* me have sex with him." I was blubbering now. "I'm so sorry for disappointing you, I—"

"Stop." She said, frowning, and warned, "Stop crying and tell me what happened, Simone." When my sobs died down she said, "Jerome threatened you how?"

I gulped and looked her dead in the eye for this one. "With the Shay's case." She averted her gaze and flexed her jaw. "Do you remember it?" I asked.

"I try not to." She said quietly.

There was a silence until she said, "What did he know?"

"The truth." I said helplessly.

My mother only shook her head and smirked at the ceiling. "I should have seen this coming. He really doesn't like your father much."

I frowned and urged, "What do you mean?

She sighed and said blandly, "A couple of years ago Zach took on the case of a teenage boy who was charged with robbery—the Cooper case. He claimed he stole a Rolex watch from a jewelry store to feed his family."

"What happened then?"

She rolled her eyes and said, "Well, your dad tried all he could to keep him,

Jerome, from going to jail, but the court did some digging around and found some old crimes he was charged with in the past. With that, they threw him in jail anyway."

Bewildered, I said, "But he was just a kid, wasn't he?"

She shook her head, "His eighteenth birthday was a week before the robbery. So, technically, no." She frowned and I thought she looked sympathetic when she said, "That poor family couldn't front the money to get him bailed out. They moved away and we never heard anything about them...till now."

Huh. So Jerome put me through all that torture because he wanted to get back at my father for putting him in jail.

I hugged my mother tightly and thanked her. I really needed to hear that, because I thought that I did something to make him hate me so much. I thought I was making everyone hate me when I wasn't. She stood and started for the door. Talk about leaving with a fresh taste in your mouth. I tightened the towel I had on and started for my bathroom when my mom's voice halted me. "Oh, and Luz wants to know if you're going with her to New York. She's leaving tomorrow."

I scowled and said, "I can't, I have school, remember?"

She widened her eyes and raised her hands in surrender, "Hey, it's not me asking. She only wants you there for the weekend..."

"Mom...?" I warned.

"Sweetie, come on. Go have fun; after all, we did miss the family reunion."

Why the hell not? As guilty as I felt for thinking it, I did deserve the fun. Besides, it would be nice to escape reality here for a while. "Don't I have court to go to or something?" Georgia told me that Jerome was going to jail and I believed that involved my appearance in the courtroom.

She shrugged, "If you're pressing charges, then yes. But he'll be in court regardless, because Gloria's not letting him get away with putting her son in a coma."

I nodded, feeling sad thinking about Seth again. However, I was determined to rid myself of the demons.

"Where is Luz anyway?" The conversation called for a major topic change. "I woke up and her side of the bed was deflated."

"She's downstairs eating lunch. Now, when you're finished cleaning come on down and eat with everyone else."

I nodded, "Okay, let me get dressed and I'll be down in a jiff."

"Okay." She said and left.

Once I finished dressing into some blue jeans and my Simply Me shirt, I decided to call Prudence, the girl I completely forgot about. When I dialed, there was a dial tone and I waited patiently until I heard Pru's calm voice. "Hello?"

"Uh, hi, is this Pru?" I asked.

She laughed and said, "Yes, who is this?"

"Oh, um, this is Simone. You asked me to meet you for dinner last week and I couldn't make it. I was just calling to ask if I could come over this afternoon for lunch."

There was a pause and I could practically hear her thinking about it. "Well, I just got home from school and I was making dinner anyway, so that would be okay."

Awesome, she didn't hate me. "Okay, when can I come over?"

A pause. "How about in a half hour, it'll give me time to clean and stuff. Oh, and I live on Patterson Street, okay?"

"Okay. See you then."

"Okay, later." She hung up and so did I when I realized Patterson Street was the projects and seriously dangerous territory.

Ah, crap.

Chapter Sixteen

We Like To Party

I drove, slowly and carefully, down Patterson Street a.k.a the projects. Thankfully, my car was restored and I could feel more comfortable driving down these streets. There were literally groups of guys dressed in dark colors and frowning at every living thing that passed them. I frowned at the deplorable sight of the houses on each block. Most were dark colored and looked as though they owned slumlords. I really considered pulling out my cell phone to call Pru and ask if she could repeat her address to me, but when I began fumbling around for it the sight of a familiar black girl caught my attention.

Pru was sitting on the tiny excuse for a porch, waving at my slow moving car. "Oh!" I said in realization and parked on the curb in front of her house. Once I got out, I noticed the paranoid stares on my way to her porch. When I climbed the steps I walked into Pru's open arms and hugged her. "Hey, girl! It's good to see you..." Her voice trailed off the second she saw my face up close. Her features were filled with concern when she added, "Oh my...girl, what happened to you? Are you okay?"

It took me a minute to realize what she was talking about, but when I did, I turned away quickly. I knew she saw the bruises there on my cheeks and jaw line, and I was ashamed of them. They only reminded me of how hard it would be to live without Seth, and how it was so much my fault. I shut my eyes tightly and said thickly, "Um, can we go inside now? It's kind of warm out here."

"Okay." She said gently, and guided me inside the small living room. It smelled like herbs and spices and the living room was tidy. There was a long couch and a rocking chair in the far corner of the room. A TV sat on a medium sized table in front of the window and playing was an advertisement for a new comedy show. "Excuse the mess, um, it usually looks pretty clean in here, but your call was so last minute I—"

I smiled a smile that I could tell didn't meet my eyes. "It's okay. It's nice in here."

She smiled appreciatively and began, "Oh, well I can take your hoodie if—" The sound of a loud engine broke off her sentence and it was followed by distant juvenile tittering. I frowned and she hurried to the door, "Oh, that's the bus!" She unlocked and opened the door and called, "Thanks Mrs. Roberts! Hey guys!" Currently, I was confused and when the distant tittering became nearing laughter I had to force myself to remember what she said all those days ago when we met in the store. She said something about having kids to raise, but I didn't regard it as anything serious. At the moment I just thought she was being dramatic because she really wanted those pants. Well, all my doubts were confirmed the instant I saw two children scurry inside and stop to stare dumbly at me. Pru was out there talking, and while doing that, there was an awkward silence between the three of us. "Hi guys." I said in an über friendly tone. They only gawked until the little girl piped up, "Who are you?"

"Uh..." Before I could explain, Pru walked in holding a little boy in her arms. Where were all these kids coming from? I was thinking that when she came from behind the little boy and girl and placed her hands on their shoulders. The baby babbled in her arms when she said, "Tristan, Shaniece, this is a friend of mine. Now y'all say hi to Simone."

"Hey." They mumbled shyly together.

I smiled and waved lamely at them. "You guys just got back from school?" At the mention of school they smiled and Shaniece said, "Yeah! And today we colored and used *paste!* Do you believe that?" I laughed and looked up at a smiling Pru. "Yeah," she answered my questioning expression. "She's quite the chatterbox." Shaniece frowned and waved her little finger in the air saying, "No, I'm not! People *like* to hear me talk, Pru."

Pru waved it away while laughing and said, "Tristan doesn't really say much, but he's very friendly, huh Tris?"

He nodded, seemingly frightened, "Uh-huh."

She rubbed his shaved head and bounced the child in her arms. "And this here is my baby boy, Aaron. His birthday was last week; he just turned one." I glanced at the little boy who seemed oddly lighter than every-one else and smiled. "He's adorable." I whispered.

"Yeah, we had *cake!* Do you believe that?" Shaniece exclaimed.

Pru and I laughed and she sent them down the hall to wash and prepare for dinner. "Four year olds—what are you gonna do?" She said to herself. I chuckled and said, "Need any help in the kitchen?"

She frowned, adjusted Aaron in her arms, and said, "Hm, well, you can help, but let me put Aaron in bed and I'll be right back." She paused, studied my face, and added, "Wanna come along? "

I shrugged, what else did I have to do? "Sure."

She led me down the hall to a small room with a bed in it. She laid Aaron on it, covered him up and kissed him on the forehead. "I'll be back to get you for dinner okay?" I heard soft babbling and she stood straight then. We walked out then and she shut the door behind her. I turned to her and asked, "So, you have three kids?"

She smiled, as if the thought of them warmed her, and replied, "Yes, I do and I wouldn't change them for the world." We entered the kitchen and I saw the origin of the herb and spice aroma in a pot on the stove. The smell was delicious and made my stomach roar; I forgotten that I'd skipped lunch.

Pru went to stir the pot's contents with a large spoon and said, "Aaron is technically my only son. I had him last year and that was around the time my boyfriend and I gained legal custody of the twins, Shaniece and Tristan." She stopped stirring and added gravely, "Our parents were killed in a drive-by last year. One minute we were in the living room watching TV and the next there were gunshots..." I could hear the strain in her voice and I was at her side in an instant. I placed a hand to her shoulder and said softly, "I may not be an expert, but I do know a little something about loss." I shut my eyes and remembered the handsome little third grader with dark hair and crystal blue eyes. How I would miss that boy... "And it's not fun." I finished, struggling with myself to find composure. Determined, however, to keep my mind off the depression I did a quick breathing exercise and clapped my hands together once. "Hey, that smells delish—what is it?" When I acknowledged the food my guts began to dissolve and my mouth started salivating. She smiled and said cheerily, "Oh, well, I don't mean to brag but it's one of the best dishes you'll ever taste. My spaghetti's the best." She looked quite smug when I teased, "Oh, yeah? I bet it's gross!" I feigned gagging noises and she turned to me. "We'll see."

That spaghetti was *seriously* not gross.

The five of us were seated at the rounded dining room table which was, ironically, the kitchen as well. Pru had finished feeding Aaron at his highchair and she stood to collect her plate. "Anybody want seconds?"

"Can I have more garlic bread, Pru?" Shaniece asked with a mouthful of noodles. Pru frowned, grabbed the end of her apron, and cleaned the girl's meat stained cheeks. "Nieceie, how many times do I have to tell you not to talk with food in your mouth?"

Once her face was cleaned, Shaniece smiled widely and sweetly said, "I love you, Pru!"

Pru rolled her eyes and went to the oven, opened it, and handed Shaniece some garlic bread. "Yeah, yeah, me too; just don't do it again."

"'Kay." She agreed happily and took a big chomp out of her bread. I smiled at the sight—the sight of a broken but happy family. They went through the wire, especially Pru, with losing both of their parents and starting over in the same dangerous neighborhood. I saw the girl in an entirely different light then, because she was probably one of the only people on earth I actually respected. Pru looked at me and said, "So, Simone, what's new?"

I wanted to laugh at that. There was so much, so much unwanted newness that I didn't think I was comfortable answering. I shook my head, "Nothing."

Her brows arched, a sly smile on her face, "Oh, really? What about with what's-his-name? Uh, Seth?"

I flinched, each time I heard his name it hurt all over. "Nothing."

"Oh, really?" She twirled her fork in her sauce and shoveled some noodles in her mouth. When she was done chewing she said, "'Cause I noticed the chemistry between the two of you in third period—and I don't mean the subject."

"Can I have some more, uh, meatballs?" She frowned in concern, nodded, and passed the bowl of meatballs on the table. "Thanks," I said and began shoveling them on my nearly empty plate. "Simone?"

I didn't answer her, just kept on shoveling.

"Simone!" She snapped and snatched the bowl from me. I did not want to meet her eyes, because I was afraid of what I would say. So, instead, I grabbed my fork and started stuffing my face. "Pru, what's wrong with Ms. Simone?" Silent Tristan asked, sounding astonished by my behavior. Pru answered him in a gasp, "Nothing sweetheart, will you guys excuse us for a minute? I need to talk to Simone."

"Okay," The twins said sadly and in synchronization before they ran back down the hall. Aaron babbled while Pru got up from her seat and kneeled in front of my chair. "Simone? What's wrong?"

I stopped eating and now tears were coursing down my face. "Simone?" She asked worriedly.

I shook my head before saying, "S-Seth is gone."

She frowned, confused momentarily, until realization crossed her features. Her eyes were glassy and she gasped, "Oh my gosh...Simone what happened?"

I gulped my fears and tears and blubbered, "He walked in on me... having sex...with..." I couldn't even bare to say it.

She shook me gently, "I can't help you if you don't tell

me what's wrong." I nodded and inhaled steadily. Once I calmed a little I was able to finish, "He walked in on me having sex with someone else and the two of them got in a fight...a bad one."

"How bad?" She inquired.

I could feel my hatred for him arise and I spat, "The bastard fucked up his brain...he's in a coma now and the doctors think that he won't make it."

I saw a single tear slip down her eye and the next thing I knew I was in her arms. It wasn't gay or anything, but it did help. We sat there for a long while with a heavy silence in the air. I would normally never condone too much thinking on my behalf, but this time they were good thoughts. Mostly thoughts of the good times with Seth. The good times...there were too many.

I was deep in thought when Pru pulled back and gazed into my eyes. I wiped the tears from mine and whispered brokenly, "Thanks, Pru...you're the best..."

Oddly, it looked like Pru...couldn't handle herself. I frowned at that and a few other things like the weird way her gaze slid from my eyes to my nose and lingered on my lips. "P-Pru, are you—"

If I had to pick any memory to erase it would be the one where Pru leaned into me and placed a hungry kiss to my tear stained lips.

Chapter Seventeen

Death By Vanilla

Her hands gravitated to my breasts and I can honestly say it took me a minute to believe it was really happening. Aaron babbled some nonsense from his highchair and Pru pulled back from my lips and panted; "I've waited so long to do this..." she gave a little moan against my lips and stood to straddle my hips.

Shit came to me then when I realized her intentions, so I shoved her—hard—to the floor. I was standing now, hovering over her on the floor, and glaring at her with disgust. "You fucking scum! What the hell was that?"

She sat up, rubbing her back and groaning from the pain, and said, "Jeez, you act like you've never had a little kiss before." She stood up and gazed into my eyes again. Automatically, her growing smile was halted and turned into a mask of apology. "Oh, I'm sorry Simone. I shouldn't have done that—"

Disgusted, I shoved her back to the floor.

"Okay, that first shove I deserved, but what was that one for?" She asked innocently. My eyes bugged in disbelief and I hissed, "That one was for doing all that shit in front of your own son. You nasty...ugh!" I exhaled sharply and added, "You know what— I'm outta here—"

"No!" Pru climbed to her feet and hugged me from behind. She was sobbing while I fought her, "Simone, please don't go! I-I love you."

I paused at that. What the hell was her problem? Did I have a sign on me somewhere that said, "kiss me I'm easy"? Oh hell to the no; I was, pardon my French, strictly dickly. When I stopped fighting her she purred in my ear, "I *want* you, baby. Think about it, I could make you so happy if—"

"*What the hell is going on in here?*" A deep, panicked, voice came from the threshold in the kitchen. I struggled out of Pru's grasp to see a tall white guy in the doorway wearing a McDonald's employee shirt—glaring at us.

"Kyle!" Pru yelped and instantly distanced herself from me.

Sensing the tension, Aaron threw his head back and started bawling. Kyle, wild-eyed, stalked over and picked up the crying baby. He was bouncing him and whispering, "There, there—don't be scared. Daddy's just about to put mommy in check. Calm down baby." The look he gave her was so full of contempt I nearly shut my eyes from it. He walked quickly down the hall and disappeared inside a room. I glanced from the hallway to the door and plotted my escape. Okay, if plotting, I meant running my fat ass out the door and to my car faster than the speed of light.

Once I got in my car I saw Kyle emerge from the house and toward my car. "You better come back here you gay bitch!"

I hit the gas and sped down the street and out of the projects. Not even caring about the serious ass whooping Pru was in for.

Chapter Eighteen

Wade in the Water, Birds in the Air

I could tell that my face was heated when I walked through the door. No doubt, my family noticed when I entered the cooking quarters. My parents were home for the day to watch over me and stuff, so they were there, along with Luz. They were sitting at the bar stools and they turned around to see me, flustered.

Luz sat her cup down and exclaimed, "Uh-uh, what's wrong with you? You been in a fight?" My father stood up from his stool, popped Luz on the back of her head, and approached me. His hazel eyes glittered and Luz shouted, "Watch yourself old man! I'm not in a good mood."

He waved her away and then put his hands on my shoulders. "Are you okay sweetheart?" Okay, I know it was a heartfelt gesture, but it bothered the hell out of me that he always thought something was wrong. Like, seriously, he should stop being so paranoid! It was irking me.

I shrugged his hands off and said, "Dad, I'm fine." I brushed passed him to get into the kitchen and toward Luz and my mother's worried gazes. Apparently, they were pissing me off too, so I raised my voice, "What?"

"Who you getting' loud with? We jus tryin to help yo ass." Luz said defensively. I rolled my eyes and got in front of her, she was so much talk. She always had something smart to say and could never back it up, always. "Luz, seriously, I'm about to punch you in the face."

She frowned and said, "And bitch if you mar my skin, there won't be a fight 'cause you'll be shot."

"Ladies!" My mother warned and placed herself between us. I backed away and put my hands to my face, confused. Why was I doing this? Barking at my family? They did nothing to me and all I was doing was pushing them away. Jeez, I was one lost cause.

I exhaled and finally looked at my family with some sanity. I realized that I couldn't keep doing this; acting like a bitch. I acted like a bitch with Seth, and he was gone, and now I was only repeating history. Not anymore, because they could easily slip away from you, or you could never see them again. To hide and retreat into your emotions and being unable to accept yourself was binding and dangerous. I guess I realized that, in order to truly love yourself you'd have to take a step in traffic and out of the cave.

"Mom, Dad...I want to tell you something."

"Yes?" The three of them looked scared now from the sudden mood swing. I couldn't blame them, I was kind of crazy.

There would be no more hiding from this one and I would be willing to accept any hardships I would have to face...somewhere else. "Well, I was letting you know that I was going to New York...with Luz."

"Yay!" Luz squealed and hugged my unmoving frame tightly. I sighed heavily and moved her gently away. She frowned and said, "Is something wrong?"

I shook my head and forced the tears from falling down my cheeks. My voice was trembling when I said, "Mom, Dad, I realized that I wanted to go with Luz to New York...to stay. I've already got my papers together and all I need to do is get there. Now, I'm not asking you, I'm letting you know that I want to move."

Everyone was silent for a long while, just looking at me with mixed emotions: shock, confusion, and understanding. I kept my gaze to the floor until my dad finally said, "Well, sweetheart, you are eighteen. So I can't tell you what to do, but...I understand if you want to do that."

I smiled faintly, "Thanks daddy."

He came over to me and gave me a hug. My mother was still in front of me when she said, "I don't want you to go. Not at all, but..." She paused and said in Spanish, "I guess you can stay with your *tia* Adriana, eh?"

I smiled full on and hugged her. There were just us in that moment but I made it a point to actually listen to what Luz had to say.

"Simone, of course you can stay with us."

I broke off from my mother's hug and hugged my annoying ass cousin. She pulled back whispered, "I've already packed up."

I nodded. "Okay, then let me get a few things and we can get ready to go." I went upstairs then with something I promised my mother I would never have: A smile on my face that actually meant something.

Chapter Nineteen

Straight To The Promise Land

We'd said our goodbyes and were pretty much out of there. My mother, of course, cried and I thought I saw my dad tear up a little too at my departure. In the passenger seat I turned to Luz; she smiled and met my gaze saying, "You ready?"

I thought about that for a moment and found the strength to answer. This was something I had to do, for me. With renewed determination, I looked her in the eye and answered, "Definitely."

"Okay," She said, started her black Range Rover to begin driving down the street. Looking back, I saw my parents waving at us and I waved back. It did sadden me that I had to move, but it was the only way I could cope with the pain of living around so many memories of the bad times and Seth. I would never see Jerome again, because I didn't press charges. I didn't wish for anyone's freedom to be taken away from them, and though it would have sounded dumb, but I didn't want to be God. I didn't want the burden of sending people to jail, the power to decide their fate.

Now I watched as the scenery blurred by and just thought. This would normally be a bad thing, but I didn't dread thinking anymore because I had a lot of positive to look forward to. Moving to New York was a wise move, I kept telling myself that over and over until I could finally get the feel of it—that what I was doing was a good thing. For me...

"Luz," I said during the drive.

"Huh?" she said. She'd been popping gum to the beat of the music that was playing on the radio. It would normally annoy me that she was doing that, but I didn't care. I just wanted to get out of Jersey as fast as I could. It was too much.

"Uh, you think once we get there you can show me around? I mean, I haven't been there in a while."

She smiled, blew a bubble, and babbled, "Girl, you don't need me. Trust me, nothing has changed since you last visited."

I shrugged, "Okay, I guess."

"'Kay." Luz said merrily once we reached a familiar looking gas station. She leaned down and got her purse, pulling out a twenty. When she got her money together, she looked up at me and asked, "Oh, you want anything while I'm getting gas?"

I shook my head (that spaghetti was still wearing on me) and I thought I felt some heartburn coming on. "Nah, I'm good. If anything, I need some Tums."

"Gotcha." She said and paced inside the store. While she was inside, I decided to surf through the radio stations until I found some Black Eyed Peas. When the most interesting thing I could find on the radio was Fergie's, "Glamorous" I decided to just turn the damn thing off. Bored and a little defeated, I leaned back on my seat and gazed out the window to see something that instantly made me cry.

Granted, across the street was Riot, the skate park Seth frequented. Instantly, I remembered the day I went to show him my horrid looking glasses (as to which, I was wearing contacts now) because I thought my parents were tyrannical. Even though that may have been a little bratty, he comforted me anyway. He comforted me even when I didn't deserve it, and thinking of all that made me feel so miserable. It also made me think about some other things, like how I couldn't just leave an untreated wound. I needed closure and the best way to do that was to confront the past to help me with my future.

When Luz finished pumping the gas into the truck, she got inside singing lowly, "Better Days" by Tupac. It wasn't strange to hear one of my most spirited family members singing a song like that, but it was only a wonder why she was in a, "Better Days" mood. Shaking it off, I grabbed the steering wheel and she yelped. "Mo, what the hell is up with you?"

"Please take me to the Washington apartments."

"Ugh, why?"

"To get closure." I huffed.

She looked unsure before she started the truck and mumbled, "You and your women's empowerment antics...I swear."

Luz knew exactly where that was, which was no surprise since she was everywhere all the time, and when we got there she pulled into the vacant lot. Everything about the place seemed dreary and dire that I almost told her to turn around and turnpike it to New York. Determined, I got out the car and started up the stairs that led to the main porch. "Mo! Where you goin'?" I could hear her panicked little footsteps running toward me. I smiled and turned to her, now in my face. "I *need* to do this, Lu, okay?"

She studied my face before she nodded. "All right, then girl—go get your justice."

I rolled my eyes and walked inside the apartment building. I was wandering down the first floor until I reached the treasured yet wretched 4A. Luz stood by my side while I watched it sadly and battled myself. I wiped the tears from my eyes and cursed myself for them. Jeez, I was always crying—I had to be strong. I had to woman-up.

"Oh for Christ sake—" Luz began and knocked on the door. I turned to glare at her and she gave me an innocent look, "What? I have to be in Queens by tomorrow night, trust me, I've missed enough school in my years."

I could definitely relate to that so I just held my tongue. Well, at least until a miniature Seth answered the door. His blue eyes were pensive and I smiled

weakly, "Hey, Code, how you holding up?"

Cody looked up at me and smiled a smile that didn't make me happy at all. I could hear Luz silent sobs beside me and I so envied her, because that's all I wanted to do lately. I knew I couldn't just breakdown though; I had to be strong for his family right now. "We're good, Sim. My mom was just making dinner, if you wanna stay or anything." The devious little boy who I was used to know was gone, and replaced by this sad, hollow creature. Again, I was so full on garlic bread I didn't even want to think about food. I shook my head and leaned down to ruffle his dark curls. "Nah, I just swung by to say bye to you guys."

Now that seemed to get him out of his funk, "Bye?"

I nodded, "Yeah, I'm moving to New York for a while."

He scowled up at me and that's when the waterworks came. "No! You can't freaking move! Are you mad at us? H-How could you do that to us?"

"Cody, it's not like that—"

"No. If you leave then you'd be leaving Seth." He swiped at his face furiously and whispered, "You'll be *leaving* him."

"Sweetheart, you have to understand that Simone's not mad at you." Luz said soothingly to him. Cody just shook his head back forth before running back inside. I sighed, feeling all bad, and walked in. I turned to the left and saw his mother in the small kitchen, frying chicken wings. Her wings were always awesome (even better than my mom's) but even though I wasn't that hungry I knew would regret turning them down later. She looked in my direction and smiled sadly. Turning her chicken once more, she wiped her hands on her apron and came over to hug me. Still smiling, she looked at Luz standing awkwardly beside me and signed, "Who's that?"

"My cousin, Luz, from New York." I signed back.

She nodded and opened her arms for Luz to hug her as well. Luz was skeptic at first, mostly because she wasn't used to such kindness in Jersey, but eventually bore through it enough to be shocked at my knowledge of signing.

She invited us into the living room, but I declined and said, "No, I just came to wish you well and say a quick goodbye."

She furrowed her brows and replied, "You're leaving?"

I nodded and smiled faintly, "Yeah, I'm moving to New York today."

She nodded, looking wistful, and signed, "Okay, will you at least visit with us soon?" I nodded and hugged her again. She was one of the very people I'd miss if nobody else. I always went to her for sage advice, or Seth, because she was the best person to talk to. Even though she was deaf, she was wiser than any other person I knew who could hear and could always sense what others were feeling.

Like now, she knew I was tense and sad about leaving. But she was the one I would expect to be understanding about my choice, because she always had that neutral way of looking at life.

There was silence for a while until I heard the sobs nearing us. When Luz and I turned around, Gloria did as well and automatically went to her crying son. Cody said out loud to his mother, "Mom, Simone's leaving us to go to New York. Can you tell her not to go? You're a grownup, so you can do that." Since Gloria was an expert at reading lips she knew what he saying and signed. "*Baby, I can't make her do what she doesn't want to do. She's a big girl and she knows what she's doing.*"

I had the distinct feeling that she was indirectly telling me not to go, but I ignored it as well as Luz whispering beside me, "Girl, you gotta' teach me how to do that sign thing, it's way cool." I elbowed her and walked up to Cody. He looked up at me and I saw the bags under his eyes. Thinking back now I wished I could forget the next words he'd uttered to me, "I just want my brother back, Sim. I just want him back..."

I couldn't help but agree with those words and have my mind made up about definitely moving to New York.

Chapter Twenty

HIGHTAILING IN A DITCH

"Simone, wake up, we're almost there." I heard Luz's drowsy voice from beside me. We'd been on the road for two hours and looking out the window now I could see the pitch black sky. I scowled from a few things: being woken up and not knowing where the hell I was. When I turned to my cousin, her eyes were weary and her curly hair was mussed. She'd just stopped at a light when I yawned, stretched and offered, "I can take over now, if you want. I mean, you look kind of tired of over there." She glanced over at me and smiled lazily. "Oh, don't worry about it; we're about ten minutes away from my place anyway. Just go back to sleep."

I shrugged and leaned back against my seat to close my eyes. Heck, I could always use more sleep. "So, what's Queens Heights like?" I asked idly, my eyes still shut.

Luz sighed and said, "Well, it's a little rough, you know all kids from the north are catty. But I manage just fine."

"Oh."

She chuckled softly, "Man, I can't wait to see Joey. I bet he's complaining that I'm not there now."

"Aw, that's cute." I said sleepily.

"Yeah. And there are a few people who can't wait to see you girl! My parents have been waiting to see you for a while." I smiled at that. I did miss my *tia* Adriana and Uncle Carlos. They were awesome because they spoiled the hell out of me when my parents weren't around. The irony of it all was that my mother, Ashleigh, and aunt, Adriana were twins and one was the fun one and the other was the responsible one. Where my mother was a tightwad my aunt was carefree. The two would always but heads when together, but could never stay apart from each other too long. My aunt told me it was a twin thing. Oh and where I was an only child, *tia* Adriana had three girls: Lolita, Liana (twins) and Luz. It was only a wonder who was the craziest out of the three of them.

I was still thinking of so many sweet memories with my crazy family when the truck stopped. Looking up, I saw that we were...hell, I didn't know. All I know is I heard the car door open and when I sat up in my seat I saw no trace of Luz. There was no way we could be at her place already; an hour didn't pass that quickly. When I glanced out my window, I saw that the truck was parked outside a very suburban looking home with a white fence and matching shutters and stuff. It was an odd sight to see in Queens, but hey, some people did manage to do it. I squinted in the darkness and saw an exhausted Luz waving at me from the front porch. "Here goes nothing," I muttered once I got out of the truck. I knew from experience that this place was not Luz's, because they'd lived in the same house and on the same street since Luz and I were born.

So, where the hell were we now?

"Luz?" I hissed fiercely to her when I reached the top of the porch steps. She looked at me and, literally, all I saw was bags under her eyes and defeat. When she spoke her words were slurred and she looked like someone drugged her. I frowned and said worriedly, "Luz?"

She nearly fainted against my shoulder, but composed herself and said, "I-I'm too tired to...just lemme' do this, okay?"

"Do what?" I demanded. Was she high?

Luz sighed dreamily and knocked on the door. "Lu, do you know where we are? Is this some sort of joke? You know people here aren't that nice!"

"Shh..." She put her hand to my mouth to silence me.

"What the—" I began, but was interrupted by the porch light and calm voice that answered the door.

"Hello?" The woman asked. She was black with wild curly hair and dressed in a nightgown. Her eyes were squinting against the porch light that was on. The woman looked entirely bewildered when I stuttered, "L-Listen ma'am, I'm sorry about this my cousin was just playing around—"

"Luz? Girl, is that you?" I looked down at Luz who was laying in my arms now and scowled. The woman looked from her to me and said, "Oh, lord tell me this girl isn't drunk?"

"How do you know—" I began.

"Eli!" The woman called inside the house. "We got a drunk one!" She shook her head and ushered for us to come inside the house. She helped me drag Luz inside and guided me to the couch, "Here, let's set her on the sofa." When we laid her down she sighed happily and started snoring. There was a silence for a moment until suddenly all the lights came on and an army of people started pouring downstairs. The lady with wild hair who opened the door said, exasperated, "Dang! I only called my husband and everyone came running down the stairs like there was a burglar down here!" A black guy, probably in his forties, came forward and looked down at Luz on the couch. He put a hand to his chest and sighed in relief, "Oh!" Then he looked pissed and told the lady, "Well you can't blame the kids for running down here Cynthia! You did sound like you fell and you couldn't get up or something."

She swatted him on the arm and exclaimed, "Oh, be quiet and go on back to bed. It was only Luz, it appears that she's drunk again, babe."

"Luz?" Everyone in the room said in surprise. Damn, my cousin got around, because as I stared at those four unfamiliar faces I began to plot my escape. Heck, I didn't know these people. They could be psychos who happened to know my cousin because they wanted her to be the final piece of their human centipede or something.

"That can't be Luz, she's in Jersey visiting family." The girl from the stairway said. Now, she looked eerily familiar but I had no idea who she was. Cynthia gestured for them to go near the couch where Luz was for proof. The young girl approached the couch and said in concern, "Oh crap—well is she okay?"

Everyone turned to me, expecting an answer. I put my hands up in surrender and said nervously, "She drove all the way from New Jersey to here; my guess is she's just tired."

"Poor thing." The young girl said and sat next to Luz. She started stroking her hair when the guy with the dreads said from the staircase. "Hey, um, quick question; who are you?"

I flinched when I realized that he was talking to me. He came near me then and got real close to my face; I backed up. He chuckled and said, "Damn, whoever you are, you look just like Luz. You her sister?"

"Language, young man..." Cynthia warned him. The dread guy just smiled sheepishly and said, "Sorry ma."

"Uh..." I began, wondering if I should give out any personal information or not. It appeared I didn't have much of a choice when the girl, I thought she was Spanish, stood from where she sat next to Luz and came near me, too. What was with these people and closeness? Did they believe in personal space? Realization struck her and she snapped her fingers and said, "Oh shit you're—"

"Language, young lady..." Cynthia warned with more conviction.

The girl said a distant, "Sorry," and began laughing. People looked a little uneasy and the dread head said, "Are *you* drunk, Ray?"

She waved him away and said, "This is Simone, Luz's *cousin*; hey girl!" She hugged me and that's when I realized who she was too. The frightened teenager I met two years ago looked...changed. Luz wasn't lying when she said I missed everything, because I could have sworn her baby daddy was Puerto Rican. I smiled smugly and said, "Oh! Hey Reina, it's been a while. How've you been?" When we parted she shared a loving gaze with guy with the dreads. Looking closely, I noticed that he didn't look that bad and felt ashamed for thinking like that. The last thing I needed was another guy to fancy.

Seemingly complacent, she raised her hand and revealed the ostentatious diamond on her finger. I widened my eyes and said, "No way..." The last I checked she hated her baby daddy's guts.

Nodding giddily she squealed, "Yes way! We're getting married after graduation and we plan to move to Philly! How awesome is that?"

I smiled, feeling so happy for her. "So you guys live together here?" I asked curiously. I remembered the time when she was only a troubled youth and scared to death to tell her family she was pregnant at sixteen. But now I saw a grown woman, happy as ever, and proud. She shook her head, "No, I live with my parents and he—" she indicated dread-head with her thumb. "Lives at the

café. We're here only for tonight."

The dread head grinned an awesome grin and slung his arm around his fiancée's shoulders. "Yeah, that's right! That smile came from me." It was random but she giggled and he kissed her on her forehead. She punched him playfully in the ribs and said, "Simone, this is Ross Nolan."

He winked and held his hand out to me. I shook it and laughed for no reason. This guy had humorous appeal that made you just want to be in a good mood. Huh, I had to give Reina points for this one. "And this is Cynthia and Eli; Ross's parents and my soon-to-be in laws."

"Hello baby—how you doin?" Cynthia greeted me. I smiled and waved lamely, and Eli, Ross's dad, spoke up, "Hey, it's great to meet some of Luz's family. Even though I did, admittedly, deem most of you guys to be as wild as she is." We all laughed, especially me because I could understand where he was coming from with that notion. After a considerable amount of chattering it finally registered to everyone that it was about twelve at night from the contagious yawning around the room. Ross stretched and said tiredly, "Well, since there's no danger, I better go back to bed. Night y'all." He said to everyone.

"Ditto." Reina agreed and followed Ross upstairs.

When it was only Cynthia, Eli, and I left there was a silence. "Okay, so it seems you'll be spending the night here, so you can take the guest room upstairs." Cynthia said kindly and guided me upstairs. "Reina wouldn't mind a roommate. Hey, Eli, can you give Luz that comforter from the hallway closet, please?"

"All right, woman!" He called from downstairs. She smiled and we continued our journey up the stairs. "So, Simone is it?"

I nodded, "Yes ma'am?"

"Are you visiting us in Queens, or are you moving here?" I had no idea why she asked me that, but I wasn't insulted. I just answered, "Um, I'm here to stay."

She nodded as we began our journey down the long hallway. I began to tell her why I decided to move here until there was a strident cry from the room beside us. I yelped and flocked to Cynthia's side, "What the hell was that?"

"I would scold you on your language, but I need to see what my son is doing wrong."

"Huh?" I asked.

"*Mommy's coming baby!*" Reina called from the room before us, ran out, and dashed to the room the baby was in. Cynthia ran to that room too, and likewise, I followed. When I ran inside I saw Ross rocking a child in his arms. Reina looked relieved when she approached him and took the baby from his arms. Ross sighed and said tiredly, "When I walked in he woke up and started fussing. I was trying to put him back to sleep but, as always, nothing worked."

"There, there." Reina said to the baby as she rocked him, "Mommy's here."

"Boy, I thought you dropped my grandchild!" Cynthia said, standing by the door. She put a hand to her heart and added, "I was ready to cuss you out, too, for that."

"Mom, why would I drop my own son? That's just not right." He said, annoyed. There were distant footsteps and then Eli's voice boomed from the doorway, "What happened!"

"He's okay, dad. He's just a little cranky." Ross looked pissed when he said, "No offense guys, but I really need some rest. Now, if you want to remain my friend, I suggest you not see me when I'm deprived of sleep."

"Oh, shut up." Reina hissed and sat the baby back inside his crib. When she stood up, she rolled her eyes and ushered everyone out of the room. "Let's go before he goes hulk on us guys." At that, we all walked out and went our separate ways. Well, all except Reina and I, since we were sharing a room. When we said our goodnights, the both of us flocked to the large bed in the center of the room and sat down. "I don't know about you, but I'm tired as hell." Reina yawned and slid into the covers. I was tired, but I wasn't, so I just sat there. After a few minutes, Reina sat up and asked, "What's wrong, you're not sleepy?" I was feeling a little depressed to tell the truth but I shrugged. "Eh, I'm good—just thinking about some stuff."

She nodded and said suggestively, "Want to talk about it?"

I closed my eyes and willed myself to trust her, because the last time I trusted someone with my feelings I ended up losing them to a coma. "Well, it's a long story if you're up for it."

She nodded, "Sure."

"Well..." And so I told her. I trusted like I never did before and spilled my guts out on the table by telling her everything that went wrong. I told her about Georgia and how much it saddened me to leave her. I told her about the horrors of Jerome Cooper and the wonders of Seth Montgomery. I told her about the ups and downs Seth and I faced throughout our lives and how we still managed to still be friends anyway. I told her numerous things; like how I was blackmailed with the Shay's case, I didn't go as far as describing it, but I did let her know how wrong it was. I think she understood when I couldn't tell her, because of her own life. She knew, probably better than I, about secrets and how important it was to keep them that way—personal. Even though keeping a secret wasn't all that good, it was just something one had to do when the moment called for it. In the midst of secrets, I told Reina about Prudence Alcott and how she tried to make a pass at me. What Prudence did was unforgiveable, and not because of her being homosexual, but the way she went about things. I thought if she would have just came out and told me she felt such feelings, I could've helped her out, hey, I could've even helped her find a girlfriend. She did me wrong by *disrespecting* me. Disrespecting the fact that I was strictly heterosexual, as well violating my space. I was around the part where I escaped the projects when Reina shook her head and said, "So, Seth is in a coma still?"

I kept my gaze lowered when I answered, I didn't want to show any emotion. "Yes."

She studied my face with an expression beyond her years and whispered, "Do you love him?"

A tear slid down my cheek at the rawness of my feelings for him and at how I wanted him back so badly it was difficult to breathe. I nodded and said clearly, "I love him."

She sat up then and crawled over to my side of the bed. Her voice trembled when she said, "I know what it feels like to be in that situation..." She hugged me and when she pulled back I asked, "You do?" There was someone who understood what I was going through?

She smiled weakly and said, "About a year ago, Ross got in a fight and it nearly cost him his ability to walk." She put a hand to her heart and whispered, "I thought he would die. I mean, the way he looked in the hospital...wasn't good, and I was beating myself up for everything that happened because I thought everything was my fault." My eyes widened at how similar we were and at how precise she was when it came to describing how I felt. I did feel as if what happened to Seth was my fault and I still do. It was only a miracle to speak to someone who actually, from experience, empathized what I was going through. Reina was gazing at her ring adoringly and continued, "I did so many things to try to deal with the pain like write poetry and run away a lot. But I realized later on that I couldn't just run away from the hardships in my life—I had to face them and take them on to truly do good. So, I did and now Ross is better and things are looking up." I watched her with so much veneration coursing through me. To think that she went through what I did and survived was a rough one to believe. Not many people were capable of dealing with so much pain.

Reina's hand gravitated to her stomach and she began to massage it and peer off into the distance, as if she were glimpsing a memory. "I was so proud when he was able to be there to see RJ's birth. I thought he would've never gotten that chance a year ago, but I'm glad I was wrong." Yeah, I pretty much realized that RJ was her second child, because Jasmine was, now that I finally remembered, Juan Cruz's. "All I need to ask you is this, before I go to sleep." Reina began. She inhaled deeply and asked solemnly, "How strongly do you feel for Seth?"

I paused at that. Why did that matter? "Very," I answered lowly. She shook her head as if whipping herself for asking such a thing and said, "Let me rephrase that—do you believe, no matter how romance novel it may sound, that your love for Seth is enough? Do you believe in Seth?"

"*I believe in him!*" I said this with conviction and all seriousness, because I know that's what he would do for me. I couldn't even count the number of times he told me that he believed in me. That was why I loved him so deeply, because he made me feel like a better person, not just some suicidal chick who needed therapy. He made me feel like I could do anything—even the most impossible, like fly. He made me feel so alive...so right...beautiful...

Reina smiled, hugged me one more good time, and slid back inside the comforter saying, "Just have faith. Night, Mo."

Chapter Twenty-One

GOLDen Beacons

3 months later

"Whew! Who's ready for *Christmas*?" My crazy *tia* Adriana gushed when she burst through the room Luz and I decided to share. I'd been living with them for a course of about three months and already I was rethinking why I moved up here at all. I loved them, but I could only take the insanity in doses.

Luz looked up from her magazine and smiled goofily at her mother, "Oh yeah!" *Tia* Adriana walked up to her daughter and they exchanged high fives before she sat on her bed. I was on my bed next to Luz's, looking up from my Chemistry homework to watch tia Adriana . She sat still for moment and alternated her glances between me and Luz. Her eyes finally decided on me and she said seriously, "Simone, you haven't seen your family in a little over three months now. You can't be that angry with them…"

I widened my eyes and said defensively, "I talked to them a few times on the phone, all right?"

She frowned and retorted, "And was it you who called them or the other way around?"

"I—" I would have replied with something sharp, but thought about that. It was them who called me and that was a few weeks ago. I wasn't trying to cast them out, but it hurt to even think about New Jersey without crying. So, straightening up I gave her and Luz my truth, "Jersey was my past. I have other things to worry about."

Luz rolled her eyes and barked, "You are the best person ever, I swear, you deserve an award."

"Shut up, Luz!" I said. "I'm *not* a bad daughter…"

"Hey, don't get mad at us because you wanna be a Scrooge." *Tia* Adriana defended. "Seriously, don't be a buzz kill."

I rolled eyes and returned to my Chemistry homework, I was failing and I seriously needed to study. I needed the motivation to pass the course and so far I didn't have any except the eagerness to move the hell out of this loony bin. I guess what I really needed was a study buddy and so far I found no one in Queens Heights that I trusted. Well, there was Reina, but we had entirely different classes. So, I remained a recluse most of the time at that school, which in reality was kind of worse than my other school, North Creston. Where people cussed me out at my old school; these people acted. There were no real arguments at Queens Heights because the students there just started swinging for no reason. It was too much craziness for me, so I kept to myself and failed Chemistry.

tia Adriana fanned herself dramatically and said, "Well, I came in here to tell you that your mom and dad have been trying to contact you for about a week now."

I ignored her and kept studying.

From the corner of my eye I saw her and Luz shake their heads hopelessly. I wasn't going to sit there and allow them to talk trash about me, and call me a bad daughter to my face. If they wanted to do that, then they could very well do it some other time— and not in my presence. "But Simone," Luz said skeptically, "It's the holidays..."

"I know." I said and finally put my notes down. I ignored the stares I received from the two of them and continued my journey out the door. I couldn't let the haters get me down, I remembered my mom saying to me. It was funny how that one saying made me miss her all the more, because I missed my parents every day. I just knew that I couldn't go back to them without wanting to stay. And staying was not an option for me. New Jersey held too many memories I didn't want to relive nor think about. So many memories of...no, I couldn't go there. I went cold turkey, not saying *his* name for three months. Of course I thought about *him*, but I forbade myself from speaking of him. I knew, just like that, how easily I could lose composure by doing it and so I refrained from it altogether. No way did I need another hindrance from my goal, which was graduating and moving far away from the north. I realized that there was nothing for me here, so I had to distance myself completely. And there weren't enough Black Eyed Peas' songs in the world to change my mind. I would make it through on my own. I would... I did feel bad though, because Christmas was in four days and it would be my first one without all of my family. We would all agree on a place to meet and we would spend Christmas Eve there, and on Christmas day we'd open presents and enjoy the rest of the day with loud music and lots of drunken fist fights. I had no idea where the location was booked this year, but I had a hunch my *tia* Adriana had something to do with it.

When I entered the kitchen, I saw my one and only Uncle Carlos at the counter making a sub. Now he was a tad bit pudgy, but a loving guy who was just as crazy as the rest of the Lopez's. He was a dentist and was very uptight about flossing and teeth hygiene. He was a weird guy, no doubt, and even right now he had a pack of dental floss beside his plate. He was very tan, which was where Luz got it from and his eyes a dark brown. He also had very curly hair that he kept in a ponytail to the back of his head. I always thought he looked like Antonio Banderas. He smiled and nodded toward the salami, "Want some?" I shrugged and went to get a plate and sub roll. Once I opened it, I began to layer my sandwich with cheese and lettuce. He nudged my arm, "Tell me what's wrong kiddo; you're never this quiet."

I shrugged and told him the truth, "tia Adriana was antagonizing me."

He paused over the mustard and said, "Huh? How?"

I layered on some bologna and answered, "She kept telling me that I should call my parents more, and basically be a better daughter." Uncle Carlos sighed tiredly and said, "Well, honey I'm not agreeing with her, but I think you should at least call to check in on them. Actually, I think it was your dad who left all those calls for you. I guess they really want to talk to you. Why don't you want to talk to them?" Once I squirted some sub sauce on my sandwich, I began resealing things, like the mustard. I was washing my hands when I said, "I'm not avoiding them or anything; I just don't want to get my feelings hurt." I turned the sink off and just stared down at my hands. "There's just so much I don't want to talk about. I don't even want to think about that stuff." I was muttering this to myself, but when a hand on my shoulder touched me it brought me back to reality. Uncle Carlos was looking down at me in concern. "Sweetheart, like I always tell Luz, just because you have a lot to deal with doesn't mean you run away. You've got to face what's bugging you in order for it to go away." I smiled at that, was I still talking to Carlos Lopez? He was never that insightful. Shaking my head I said, "Where'd that come from? I never thought I'd see the day you'd be so serious."

He patted my shoulder and pursed his lips, "Well, that came from experience and a number of Disney Channel movies." He pause and laughed. "Those things will teach you some life lessons."

I laughed and punched him playfully on the arm. "Thanks, Uncle Carlos."

He smiled and leaned down to kiss my forehead. When he walked back to the countertop, he grabbed my sandwich, took a big bite, and said, "May the force be with you, Mo," Before he danced out the kitchen and into the living room.

Chapter Twenty-Two

Keep HOLDING On

So far, Christmas vacation was taking a bunch of turns. Lolita and Liana were home for the holidays and the, "Big Day" was tomorrow. The Bid Day was Christmas Eve and the location for the party was still a secret. Or at least, I didn't know it. The house was very busy with house decorations and Christmas wrappings and chatter. I mean, there was a bunch of conversations going on and I was the only one in the corner wrapping toys and stuff for the next day, silently. Lolita came over to me then and greeted, "Hey Mo, what's up?" I smiled half heartedly and said, "Merry Christmas, Lo." The twins looked like older versions of Luz and younger ones of Adriana . In truth, they all looked like creepy clones of each other and everyone got them mixed up. Not me though, I've lived the insanity for too long to get them confused. And besides, Luz made her identity known with her loud ass mouth. Liana came over then and said happily, "Mo! Merry Christmas, it's been too long."

"Same here, Lili." A white guy came from behind her and hugged her. He began kissing her on the neck and cowered away with a yelp. "Ouch!" He said.

Uncle Carlos came from behind him looking evil and stretched the dental floss he had in his hand around his neck. "Do that again and your head is mine, *hombre!*"

"Okay, okay, I won't." He said.

Liana called after her father, "Thanks for ruining my life dad!"

"No problem baby girl—any time." He answered from the kitchen. Yeah, Liana invited her boyfriend over for Christmas without remembering just how crazy the family was. She turned to him and watched the guy lovingly, "Don't worry Michael. My dad's not all that right in the head."

He nodded nervously and from all the way in the back of the house I could hear Luz's loud voice, "Simone! I need you to come with me to run an errand." Luz pattered into the living room with boxes in her hands and yanked me up from my seat on the sofa. Lolita glared at Luz and stood to hover over her. "Lu, you can't just take Simone like that. She's *our* cousin, too, you know?"

"Ditto." Liana said, cuddling with a nervous looking Michael.

"Well, who's her favorite? None of you guys, so back off." She snatched me and we ran for the door. In her hand, she had two big boxes and she threw one at me and said, "Run! Hurry before they catch us." I did, grateful for her interference for once, and ran for the truck. She unlocked the doors and we both got in, tossing the two big boxes in the back seat. The twins were running down the porch steps calling for us to come back as Luz made dust down the street. I was in my jammies and totally not dressed to go out. My hair was in a sloppy ponytail and I was frowning at the situation. Luz was dressed similarly and it only made me even more curious. "Lu, where are we going?"

"Trust me, girl. You won't regret it." I had a feeling I was going to, but remained silent. If we were going back to the Nolan's place then I was fine with that. Besides, I liked them, and they made me feel sort of welcomed. "Hey," Luz said to me as she sped down the street.

"Want to know where the Christmas party's being held at?"

My curiosity was gnawing at me, but I couldn't let her know that. I didn't like giving her the upper hand and plus, I wasn't really looking forward to this Christmas. It was such a small one. I shook my head, "Not really, why?"

She shrugged and said, "Huh, I just thought you wanted to know."

"Well, I don't." I said.

"Fine." She said, totally unfazed.

I wondered what was going on with people lately, everyone was trying to talk to me and give me life lessons. Like I needed saving or something. Anyway, we drove in silence until we reached another suburban looking house on the corner. It was down the street from a convenience store called, Reyes, and from then on I think I put the pieces together. There were quite a few cars parked in the driveway and on the curb that I worried we were interrupting something. After all, the Reyes's weren't really our family, so I didn't want to interlope on their day. When Luz parked, she got out and shut her door. I got out too, and helped her unload the backseat with the boxes.

The boxes weren't that big, but I was short as hell and it was a little difficult for me to walk up to the porch steps. Did everyone have long porch steps up here, or was I tripping?

Luz was standing in front of me and she knocked on the door. "Hello! Open the door people; I know you're in there!"

A short Mexican man opened the door and shook his head at Luz. "You should really invest in a muzzle, Luz." He laughed at his own joke and Luz and I made our way inside the houseful of people. "Keep it up old man and the next thing you'll see in that gift box are some *Depends*."

"Oh, you got jokes?" He said once he came back from the door. Everyone was watching us, smiling and saying in jumbled synchronization, "Hey Luz!" "Luz, you're crazy!" "Merry Christmas y'all" "Hey Simone!"

A tall handsome Spanish guy came up to me and took the box from me, "I'll take that, if you don't mind Simone?"

I frowned, "Do I know you?"

He grinned boyishly and said, "So you don't remember Reina's big brother, eh? Jeez, and I thought I was irresistible back then. I guess not." He laughed and went back to sit beside a short black woman who was holding baby girl in her arms. He leaned down and kissed her on the lips. She shook her head at him and said, "You just gotta' show off, huh, Ricky?" He started to do a little dance and sang, "Oh, you know it, boo!"

"Yeah, you should really stop dancing Enrique; I think you're making baby Emma cry." Luz said jokingly from beside me.

"Shut up, Luz!" He said and stuck his tongue out at her. Everyone laughed and I glanced around the room to get my bearings. There were many people there: Enrique and his family I supposed, Reina's parents, Juan and some white girl, and Ross was sitting next to Reina's mom, who was holding RJ, laughing about something. I leaned over and whispered in Luz's ear, "Hey, where's Reina?"

"There she is!" "Aw she's so cute!" "Such an angel" "Happy birthday baby girl!" People were saying around me when I looked up to see Reina in her pajamas, holding Jasmine in her arms walking down the stairs. She was wearing a frilly pink dress and was rubbing her eyes. It looked as if she just woke up and just entered her own birthday party. "Oh yeah," I mumbled to myself. I remembered Luz said something about

Jasmine's birthday being on Christmas Eve, which was tomorrow.

Luz, still clutching the box in her hand, ran over to them and said, "This is for my god daughter's birthday! Here!" She thrust the box in Reina's face and Jasmine laughed while trying to hold it in her little arms. Enrique took it and sat it down by the Christmas tree near the window. There were a plethora of gifts under that tree and for some reason it made me giddy. Christmas always did bring out the child in me. Everyone began singing the Happy Birthday song to Jasmine, and the babies in the room began screaming to rhythm. After the song was sang Luz hugged Jasmine a thousand times and said, "Oh, this is gonna make me cry! Well, too bad we can't stay too long—I just came to make sure everyone could make it to the Christmas Eve party tomorrow morning at the stream. You guys are game, right?"

Everyone began to speak in unison and look awkwardly away. Luz held her hand up and said, "You guys better be there or I'm going to jail tomorrow."

At that, the entire room combusted into giggles and laughter and Reina said from the stairwell, "It was a joke, Luz. Chill out and get into the Christmas spirit."

She put a hand to her heart and said, "Christmas spirit my butt, you guys better be there at Eleven thirty a.m. *Comprende?*"

"*Comprende!*" Everyone said in sync.

"Awesomeness! Now it's time to go, say bye Mo." She told me and I did. "Bye guys!" They said from inside and the next thing I knew the two of us were in the truck, preparing for a Christmas Eve full of "Awesomeness".

Chapter Twenty-Three

Deadly Calm

"Wake up, Mo! It's Christmas Eve!" Luz said, shaking me out of my awesome slumber. I had half a mind to slap her, but she moved away too fast. I sat up in bed and scratched my hair, which was extremely unkempt. My breath tasted horrible and all I wanted was to go back to sleep. I glared at Luz fluttering around the room, getting her presents together and checking them twice to make sure they're all there. "Mo, come on wake up, it's about time to go and you're the only one who's still in bed. Aren't you a *little* excited?"

I yawned and said, "Meh, kind of."

She waved my answer away and went about her inventory. I rolled out of bed and trudged into the bathroom down the hall. Once I stripped, I got in the shower and washed. This day would be one I would remember forever, because most of my family would not be with me. Or at least the family that I wanted to be here. It was a sad Thanksgiving without them already—and I wasn't one to beg, but if they could at least make an appearance....even as I thought of the possibility I knew it would stay that way—not real. I pissed my parents off by not keeping in touch with them and now I was sure they hated me. I was almost back to that point of hating myself, too. It would be incredibly ironic considering that being the reason I moved to New York in the first place.

When I finished my shower, I wrapped up and scurried on back to the room. When I got there, however, I was met by the Lopez clones, having a good old chat. "Ah!" I yelped and turned back to return to the bathroom but was caught by the twins from behind. "Hey!" I screeched as I fought the twin power that confined my arms in place. *Tia* Adriana ran to the door quickly to shut and lock it. All of this was disconcerting me and I was feeling some kind of way. "I'm sorry to do this to you sweetie, but for real, you need a makeover." I glared the shit out of my aunt and spat, "I am so gonna get you guys back—"

"Anyway," Luz said authoritatively with her arms folded across her chest. She was wearing a long knee length crocheted dress. It was red with stitched on Christmas trees on the rim and the ensemble was completed with dark green leggings. Her hair was in an up-do and she was wearing red lip coloring. Looking around me, I saw that all four of the Lopez girls wore the same thing. Once I struggled from the twins grasps I frowned at their matching attire. Luz pursed her red lips, "Yeah, you can't go to the party in that thing." I looked down at myself and yelped, "I'm wearing a towel!"

"Yeah, yeah, yeah." She said and snapped her fingers at the twins. Lolita revealed a red crocheted dress with Christmas stitching and Liana a pair of dark green leggings. The three of them began to mob around me and I widened my eyes at what was about to happen.

They were going to make me Barbie.

"No!" I hollered once I saw the devious look on their faces. How dare they make me into the very thing I mocked! tia Adriana pulled out an old friend I hadn't seen in a while from behind her and clamped the plates together saying, "Simone, meet Mr. Flat Irons."

I would have protested further had I not wanted my hair done so badly. Hey, what would a little makeup hurt?

"You look *awesome* Simone!" Michael cried once I was finally dressed and walking down the stairs. Liana elbowed him in the ribs. He yelped and rubbed the attacked part of his body, "Oh, I meant, yay Simone."

"Mm-hm." She said and folded her arms across her chest.

I rolled my eyes once I finally reached the first floor. I smiled awkwardly and said stiffly because of the lipstick, "Thanks guys, but I'm sort of a tomboy if you haven't noticed. Lipstick and six inch heels aren't really my thing." I could feel the breeze on my neck from the absence of hair there. My hair was straightened and in a high ponytail—a waterfall Luz had called it—and a bang. I had Christmas tree earrings on and my movements were extra hesitant. The Lopez clones were waiting for me with smiles on their faces.

Tia Adriana spoke first, "Oh, darling you look so wonderful!" She hugged me and I tried my best not feel like shit. This was supposed to be a good day, I told myself. A day full of laughs, and people, and gifts, and music. Yeah, this would be good. Good...good. I willed myself to chant that until it became reality. I was determined not to disappoint any more of my family, because I was striving to emerge from the cave, not retreat within it.

Nuh-uh, no more of that. I had to be a big girl and go on through this holiday without my parents.

Uncle Carlos was dressed in a neat crocheted sweater with Frosty the Snowman on the front.

When he came up to me he linked his arm through mine and said, "Cheer up *chica*, you'll have the time of your life, I swear." He promised as everyone made their way out the door. He opened the door to Luz's Range and I got in, smiling, because he always knew just what to say when I was depressed—which was most of the time. The cars were packed to their full capacity with presents. It was a tight fit, but we all managed to adjust and hit the road. I was in the passenger seat alongside Luz. Her parents were riding in their Sedan and the twins had their own cars. My car was still in Jersey and my mother said she wouldn't send it, because she felt it was my responsibility since I was on my own now. She was such a tightwad.

"So, Mo, if you had one wish for this Christmas, what would it be?"

I smiled dreamily and told her what I felt, "I would wish that all of the people that I loved would be at the party. Just...it would be great if I could see them for at least one more time."

Luz nodded and said simply, "Huh, good wish."

The rest of the drive was silent, and Luz drove extra carefully since the snow was falling in buckets. The others were following us, because most of them had no idea where the stream was. I did, because I went there almost every day after school for hot coffee and soup. Reina was the waitress there and she would spot me extra clam chowder whenever I'd order it. I think I would need some for right now, because my nerves were shot. I was jittering from the anticipation when Luz parked the car in front of the stream. "We're here! And it looks like everyone else is too!" I looked out the window to see a *bunch* of faces. Most of them I recognized as my family; the rest as friends, and then some. There was music playing and it sounded like everyone was having a good time even though it was around eleven in the morning. I was excited for some reason when I rushed out the truck. Well, too bad for me, there was ice on the ground and I was wearing heels. When I hit the ground I thought I heard a ringing through my ears and my face felt hot. "Shit, are you okay?" I heard Luz say beside me. Once she helped me up I snatched the heels off and tossed them into the street. "Hey! Those things were expensive!" She muttered and helped me inside the building. I sighed happily at the heat that welcomed me; "Merry Christmas!" The crowd sang. I smiled, despite the pain in my cheek, and sang back, "Merry Christmas everyone!" I think I disconcerted everybody with the matched enthusiasm. I could tell they were used to the uneasy or depressed Simone, because I was. They cheered, "Merry Christmas" to every person that walked through the door. The place was closed off due to the party and there was an extravagant tree that stood at the back of the stage. The song re-sang by Chris Brown called, "This Christmas" was playing softly in the background and the usual vanilla scent (Mrs. Nolan was obsessed with it) wasn't as strong as it normally was. I scanned the crowd in hopes of seeing my parents and, no surprise, they weren't there. Well, I guessed I deserved it since I was such a Godzilla of a daughter. "Simone!" I heard Luz call from beside me. I turned with a questioning expression and asked, "What?"

There was a guy a little taller than her smiling goofily with his arm slung around her neck. "This is Joseph Corazon. Joey, this is Simone; one of my favorite cousins."

He extended his hand out to me and said, "It's a pleasure." I shook it and smiled back at him, not really meaning it. Even though I vowed to myself that I wouldn't get sad I couldn't help it. It downright hurt to see that my parents weren't here for such an important event. I mean, did they love me anymore? Did they think I didn't love them? If they did, then they were so wrong. I loved them so much and needed them, especially now...dealing with the holidays like this was...insufferable. I conversed with a number of other people like Reina, Ross, Enrique, Angela (who was a very nice person), Juan (briefly), and lots of others. I was just finishing my conversation with my Uncle Gregory about the importance of Black Eyed Peas songs when Ross announced from the stage, "Merry Christmas y'all!" He was holding RJ in his arms and people were cooing all over and making baby noises.

"Merry Christmas!" Everyone yelled back.

"All right, now y'all know that this wouldn't be a Nolan Christmas without expression, and we don't know about y'all, but that's how we get down!" There were nods and words of agreement and he continued, "All right, so I'm just gonna cut right to it—who wants to do a slam?" There were shouts and he adjusted his son in his arms and said to him, "Little man, who do you think should do the slam?" The baby babbled and smiled at Reina. The lights inside the café was dim except for the spotlight that shown suddenly on her, "Ooooh!" He dribbled. Everyone melted at that and Ross laughed and said to the crowd, "Why of course he chose his mom, such an easy decision to make." Reina handed Jasmine over to me and went up to the stage. She was wearing a green sweater and some blue jeans. Her hair was a mess of long curls that were thrown back and styled with a headband. She hugged Ross and kissed RJ on the cheek before they exited the stage. She beamed at everyone and said into the microphone, "Even though I've done this a bunch of times I still get nervous. Here goes nothing." Reina's expression changed from happy to serious in an instant, and suddenly soft music began to play.

There is no doubt about it

No doubt at all

That you'll always be there

Even when the winter crawls

There will never be doubt

No doubt when I say

That I know that you're coming

I never doubted each day

I remember the times

When I try not to like

But it was all in vain

My emotions I couldn't contain

Ardor became too spiked

I would like to go to back

That's probably the most I care about

I try to get through the forces

But now I really am starting to doubt

I just wish you were here

So I can let you know

Exactly how much I care

Her words were compelling and I saw why she began to write poetry in her spare time, the girl could paint a picture. The crowd roared and she said breathlessly, "Thanks you guys! Merry Christmas and happy birthday Jasmine!" At the mention of her name, Jasmine began to wriggle in my arms, trying to dance. Reina walked up to me and held her hands out for her daughter. I handed her over and said near Reina's ear, "Uh, Ray I need to ask you something!"

There was so much noise going on she squinted her eyes in concentration and yelled, "What did you say?"

I could feel the pains in my stomach begin to gnaw at me and I believed it be my monthly visitor. My stomach was aching when I said, "Do you have any tamps I could borrow?"

She frowned, apparently not hearing what I was saying.

I sighed and screamed, "Can I borrow a tampon!" The room quieted for some reason, and the entire roomful of people turned their shocked gazes at me. My heart sped up from the embarrassment and I heard Jasmine repeat, "Tampa!" I expected laughter, but there was none, only shocked and disgusted gazes. Reina leaned into me and whispered, "Don't worry, just go upstairs into the apartment and there should be some under the sink. Hurry up, I'll distract them."

"Thanks," I said and ran for the back and up the stairs. I could hear Reina begin a speech about the importance of Christmas and I was grateful for it, because currently I wanted to die. Jeez, that was the most humiliating thing that's ever happened to me. I mean, oh my gosh...

The apartment door was unlocked and I searched the small place for a bathroom and found one near the kitchen. It was funny how; once I sat on the toilet I realized it was only gas and no menstruation. So I embarrassed myself over something that wasn't even there...that was so me. Huh, I guess it was all the eggnog. When I finished doing my business I washed my hands and just stared into the mirror, gazing at myself. There, I saw beauty for a change and I finally understood what Reina was telling me. I couldn't just erase what happened all those months ago with Seth and Jerome away, but I had to confront them to truly begin a healing process. When I stared at my reflection I saw a mask of makeup, so I cupped some water in my hands from the sink and splashed it on my face.

All of that wasn't me, but what I was trying to become to make my family happy. I remembered Seth saying somewhere in the past that he loved my hair curly, and so I let my ponytail loose and wet it. When I shook my hair out, it was in dark ringlets that flowed down my arms and past my shoulders. I smiled at the sight, this was what I liked. This was me and this was how I would stay...me. I was thinking of how I would go about my plans for a healing process when I opened the door to find a tall guy with dark hair and blue eyes staring down at me, looking confused and awestruck.

No...it couldn't be...

"Seth..." I whispered and eased back inside the bathroom. Thank goodness for Airwick, because he would have received the shock of his life had he been there the second I finished.

"S-Simone? Are you Simone?" He asked nervously. My eyes watered at that. I knew it—I was officially going crazy. Seth wasn't coming back...that couldn't be him... oh shit; I knew living with Luz for too long would have side effects. But damn, this was one hell of a hallucination. I shook my head back and forth and stuttered, "Y-You're not supposed to b-be—"

"I know it's you. I've had so many dreams about you, and my mom told me they were memories, but I wanted to see it for myself. Y-You're Simone." He was saying it over and over like he was trying to decipher the reality of it. I was fully crying now and clutching the doorframe like a lifeline. When I decided this was real, I loosened my grip and eased out of the bathroom. I was standing in front of him now looking up into those cool blue eyes that I went so long without. So he came out of his coma and...he was alive.

He was alive.

Seth was *alive*.

It didn't seem real to me, and I swore my Uncle Carlos had spiked that eggnog until Seth put his hands through my damp hair and said, "God how I've missed you." I saw the tears coursing down his cheeks as he went on, "M-My doctor said my memory should return to me in doses, but I remember so much of...you. I-I think I love you, Sim. No, I *know* I love you." His hands were still massaging my hair and I blubbered, "W-When did you wake up, Seth?" Because if I had known, my ass would have *ran* back to Jersey.

He frowned and said, "I woke up about three months ago. And ever since then, my mom says she's been trying to contact you. She told me you moved here, and my doctor just confirmed yesterday that I could travel. But even if he didn't give me the okay—I would have still came anyway. I had to see you, Sim. I love you." I hugged him hard and he nearly fell back, but I made sure he stayed upright. No way was I letting my Seth get hurt again...never again. There were so many thoughts running through my head, but mostly good ones. I was so overwhelmed that I had him back that I clung to him for a good ten minutes in silence. "I've felt so miserable without you..." I whispered. He tilted my chin up to him and leaned down to kiss me on my forehead. He smiled bravely and said, "I don't even remember how to sign anymore...now I have to talk to my mom with a pad and pencil."

"I'll teach you." I said without hesitation. I'd do anything for him just about then. He kissed me on my nose and I said, "Are you sure you remember me?"

He chuckled and said, "Why, how could I forget? You're all Cody talks about anymore. I see you've made quite the impact on my family, Sim."

I frowned at that. I didn't want to intrude on his life or anything. And if anything, I impacted his family's life for the worse. "Hey," he said and pecked my lips. "Stop worrying; I've done enough of that while you were gone."

I smiled, really smiled, and responded, "I can't help myself—you're worth it babe." I guess I was too caught in the moment to realize one major thing, and when I did I couldn't help but ask, "How'd you get here?"

He kissed me again and said, "Your aunt told your parents where the party was gonna be and they told us and...now we're here." My heart stopped at that. This was too much to be true. "My mom and dad are here?"

Seth nodded, smiling like the third grader I remembered, "Yep. You know they wouldn't miss something like this...neither would I...that's why I snuck up here...Sim, I had to see you and I just couldn't wait anymore. I just...I need to hold you right now."

I nodded vigorously and held him as tight as I could. I could feel that he'd lost weight since the last I saw him and, of course, I worried. I didn't want him unhealthy or not right or not here. I needed him to be Seth and I was determined to keep him, that major part of me, alive and well for the rest of my life.

For the rest of our lives.

It was not enough to feel his arms around me. Though I did feel secure, I wanted to be a part of him completely and so I decided to do this, something I never thought I would or could do in my life. I broke away from him and walked to the door. The hopeless look he gave me made my heart hurt, "Sim...?"

I held my hand up to silence him before I locked the door. He looked extremely bewildered when I took my dress off and shimmied out of my leggings. I put my hands on his chest and asked him with tears in my eyes, "Seth, will you make love to me?" He wiped the tears from my face and kissed me gently on the lips. When he pulled back, he said, "No, Sim. I don't want to take advantage of you. I didn't come here for that, I—"

"Shh..." I placed my hand over his mouth and whispered, "I love you Seth, and no matter what happens nothing will ever change that. Now I'm asking you as a friend, as someone who loves you...will you make love to me?"

I expected him to reject me again, because he was always just that chivalrous, but to my surprise he leaned down and whispered against my lips, "*Anything* for you babe. Anything...I love you Simone Randon."

I kissed him and said, "I love you Seth Montgomery." He picked me up, cradling me in his arms and kissing me all the way to the large bed in the center of the next room. I did feel sort of guilty for doing this on Reina's bed, but no way was I ashamed. I was doing this for Seth; to be near him. And to be away from him so long was agonizing. I think she would understand when I told her later, but right now I was relishing in the feel of Seth and how he felt so a part of me right then. It was truly one extended moment of bliss as our breathing, bodies, and spirits became one and a moment I wouldn't trade for the world.

When we finished, I laid atop his chest and said brokenly, "Don't ever leave me again Seth. Ever..."

Seth inhaled and lifted me higher so I could reach his lips. The kiss he gave me let me know that everything was going to be all right and that whatever happened later on, in our future, we'd face it together and overcome it. He massaged my hair while he breathed, "Oh Sim...you're my girl now, and you always will be."

EPILOGUE

Graduation day...

SETH

Seth Montgomery waited anxiously in his seat for Principal Clark to announce his name. He had spoken with his counselor and made a deal that he would cram and take online classes to graduate with his class. Ever since the coma, it had been hard enough to remember most of his subjects, but in time he managed to relearn it step by step and with much needed help: Simone Randon. Though his mother and brother did help him study through the nights, Simone re taught him everything he needed to know from Algebra I all the way to Calculus. He'd always remembered Simone being great with that stuff, and he appreciated it, because without her assistance and sacrificed free time he would've never made it. Now, as he sat in the booth alongside his classmates, everyone dressed in caps and gowns, he almost twitched from the suspense. He felt a small hand grab his and he nearly yelped from his shot nerves. "Stop worrying, Seth." Simone whispered from beside him. She was wearing her graduation attire as well, and he was thankful that she decided to transfer back to North Creston for this. Though he did feel like a hindrance from her dreams for having her do that, he smiled through it and reassured himself that she did it for her. Even sitting down Simone was dwarf-like, and he looked down at her and grinned, "I'm just nervous, Sim. That's all."

She laughed lowly and nudged him in the arm, "Cheer up kid, you'll do great. I promise. Look at how many people came to support you." Seth, unwillingly, averted his gaze from her and watched the audience. His mother, Gloria, was there with his brother Cody. Around them was most of his family who he hadn't seen in a while or couldn't remember. He knew they were a part of the Montgomery's though, because almost everyone of his kin owned dark hair and blue eyes. When he and his mother's gazes locked, she smiled up at him and mouthed, "I *love you*."

He signed, "I *love you, too*," to her. Oh yeah, Sim had taught him sign language again. Well, she'd shown him the basis of it and he pretty much memorized the rest. His doctor told him that it was a miracle that he couldn't comprehend that won him his memories back. Seth thanked God every day for the blessing and cherished every day he had with the ones he loved most. Speaking of one in particular, he had something planned for her after the ceremony that he knew she'd love.

If only the damn principal would call his name...

"Dana Caldwell..." Seth waited.

"Heidi Macon..." Seth's heart sped.

"Pete Samson..." Seth fidgeted.

The principal studied the paper and continued, "Simone Randon..."

"Oh *hells* yeah!" Seth sprang from his seat and hugged the hell out of Simone. Everyone laughed from the audience and she giggled in his arms. He couldn't contain himself—he was just so proud of her. She'd been through so much and to succeed through it all was so amazing it brought tears to his eyes. Simone smiled up at him, winked, and went to claim her diploma before she sat down on the other side of the stage.

"Theodore Nelson," Seth took a deep breath.

"Tasha Peyton," Seth twitched.

"Seth Montgom—" At the mention of his name, Seth stood and dashed for his diploma. "Mr. Montgomery, one more outburst from you and—"

Seth hugged the old coop and kissed him on the cheek. "Thanks man!" He patted him on the back, swaggered over to the other side of the stage, and sat on the empty seat next to Simone. He hadn't noticed how the entire audience was falling from their chairs in laughter at his behavior because all he was concerned with was that diploma and being with his Sim.

Simone reached over and hugged him, "I'm so proud of you baby." Seth had half a mind to throw his girlfriend over his shoulder and walk out of there, but decided against it at Principal Clark's nasally voice, "As always, we are extremely proud of our graduates, and will miss each and every one of your unique personalities." At the mention of that, Principal Clark gave Seth a pointed stare. Seth shrugged and said, "What? I was overwhelmed?"

The principal laughed along with the crowd and continued, "As we are, to see such talented minds depart from North Creston and go on to prosper in their brilliant futures, wherever it will take them. So, without further ado, congratulations graduates!"

"Whew!" The students stood and roared as they threw their caps into the air. There were people everywhere, but it wasn't so hard to spot Seth's blue-eyed crew. He was holding Simone's hand tightly as he made his way into his mother's arms. "*I am so proud of you sweetheart! Good luck in college this fall!*" She signed and Seth hugged her again. They were both crying and Simone waved her arms in the air saying, "Attention tall people! I need love to!" Gloria leaned down and hugged the girl and signed for her to have best wishes in college. Cody was about her height now, if not slightly taller, so he laughed and gave her a nooggie. "Congrats, Sis." He said before Seth chuckled and put him in a chokehold. "Nobody gives my girl a noogie except me, Code. Sorry dude." After that, Seth leaned and lifted Simone in his arms, wanting to do that all day, and kissed her. She moaned and pulled back from him, "Seth, not now." She was blushing bright red and that made it even more difficult for him to set her back on ground. She smiled at him and purred, "Maybe later..."

He grinned and said, "I knew I loved you for a reason, Sim!" She elbowed him and her smile fell when she seen the tears in his eyes, "Don't cry, babe. Even though we won't be attending the same college, we can still visit each other." Simone had been obsessing to get the both of them into the same college, but there had been no word so far of his acceptance. She would be attending Duke in the fall where Seth was accepted to numerous other colleges he hadn't decided on yet. He hated to leave Sim, but he had to go to school to better his future. Simone understood, and that was part of why he loved her so entirely. Seth damned himself for crying and cleared his face, "I was crying because I felt so grateful to have you, Sim."

She stood on her toes and kissed him on the cheek. "You're like, the best boyfriend *ever!*"

"Can we get some love too?" Mr. Randon's voice came from behind them. Seth instantly separated from Simone and extended his hand to the attorney. "Um, I apologize— hello Mr. Randon." He only looked at his hand and slapped it away. Mr. Randon put his hand on Seth's neck and grabbed him in a very manly hug. "Don't apologize to me, young man. This is your day!"

When they pulled apart Mrs. Randon hugged him and cried, "Oh, my babies are leaving me! Oh gosh..." Mr. Randon pried his wife from Seth, "She'll be all right after a few drinks. Don't worry about her."

Seth laughed.

Simone said her thank you's and hellos to her parents before some black girl came up to her and said, "Congratulations, Mo!" Oh, he knew who that was. Even though he'd only met her a few months ago, she was quite the character to never forget. Simone embraced her cousin and said gaily, "Thank you, Luz! I appreciate that!"

"No *problemo!* And you," She indicated Seth with her index finger.

He grinned, "What?"

"You better give me hug before I swing! Acting like you couldn't say hi to me!" Seth rolled his eyes and hugged her. Her humor was weird, but funny, and that's why he enjoyed her company. "Y'all *better* be there for my graduation in a month, or I'll be coming for you!"

"All right, Luz." The two said in unison. They broke off into a heated conversation about whose graduation would be better until a black girl with long braids walked up to Simone and asked, "Simone?"

Simone's smile fell and Seth was immediately on guard. He didn't want anybody to ruin this day for her, shoot, he fought for her before and would do it again in a heartbeat. She only had to say the word...

Simone smiled sadly and said, "Hey Georgia. How's it going?"

The girl nodded and said, "Things are fine. I just came to wish you congratulations." A tear slid down her cheek and she said, "You were one of my best friends Simone." Simone's eyes misted, too, and she opened her arms and said, "Oh come here! I know it's killing you that you didn't call me Momo."

She laughed and hugged her. "Thanks, Momo! I was so scared that you were mad at me."

Simone shook her head and said, "You don't deserve my anger when all you did was be my friend, especially when I needed one. Thank you, Georgia."

"You're welcome!" She exclaimed.

Seth looked at Luz and mouthed, "Who is she?"

Luz grinned and waved it away mouthing, "A *friend*." Seth nodded and gave her the thumbs up. Well, it was best to do this now before he chickened out. Since Luz knew what he had planned, she slung her arm around Georgia's shoulders and said, "Walk with me freshman..." At that, the two of them walked away and Simone frowned up at Seth. "What was that?"

"Oh, nothing." He took her by the hand and led her to the big oak tree that secluded the two of them from the rest of the parents and graduates. Simone looked completely concerned then and asked, "Seth, what's going on? Is this some kind of j—?"

"Shh..." He said as he kneeled down on one knee before her. Tears automatically came to her eyes and she placed a hand over her mouth whispering, "Seth, you didn't—"

"Simone, I love you and I can't even imagine a day without that beautiful face of yours in it. So, as a token of my love for you..." He pulled a wide, flat, case from his robe and opened it to reveal something he was sure she'd freak over.

Simone screamed. "Oh my gosh! Y-You got accepted into Duke?" Seth nodded and pulled the entire acceptance letter from the case and recited the first sentence to her, "We are glad to inform you, Seth Montgomery, that you meet our standards and hope to see you this fall at Duke University. Congratulations." Simone was blubbering then, "Oh, Seth I'm so happy for you—you deserve everything—I love you so much..." Seth kissed her then and the two of them began walking to the parking lot. Simone was quiet the entire walk and Seth had to ask, "You okay, Sim?"

She nodded, "Y-Yeah, why wouldn't I be?"

He shrugged and when they reached her car he frowned and said, "Oh, because I was thinking that maybe we could get married sometime later. What do you think?"

Simone squealed before she fainted against him. Seth laughed as helped her up, and knew that as long as he lived he would do the same every time she fell. Whenever she fell down, he'd help her up and out of the cave that once claimed her for the worse.

Always.

LUZ

Luz was so proud of her cousin. She'd been through so much and deserved this day entirely. It seemed like yesterday when she moved into the Lopez's house and turned everyone's life around. Simone hadn't noticed it, but wherever she went she changed people for the better. She only wished her cousin the world and to have fun.

Luz said her goodbyes to Georgia and flocked on over to her family. Her mother, Adriana , was arguing with her twin sister, Aunt Ashleigh. The two always found something to fight over while their husbands stood and watched silently in the background. Looking around, she spotted her twin sisters, Lolita and Liana arguing over a jacket and smiled at the sight. Wow, this was her crazy family and no way would she exchange them for anything. She fit just right in the pandemonium. After all, she was known to everyone as the craziest of them all. And Luz took pride in that.

Suddenly parched, she sauntered over to the dessert table and poured herself a glass of punch. However, she saw a bee hovering angrily over the bowl and flinched away from it—the punch in her hand hitting the graduates brand new gown. He yelped and she placed a hand over her mouth. "I am so sorry!" She grabbed one of the napkins from the table and began to swipe the red juice from his royal blue gown. "Oh, I saw a bee and I freaked out—oh, I am such a damn klutz—"

The guy smiled brilliantly and chuckled, "It's okay, slow down! Don't worry about this thing, it's just a dress." He stopped wiping his gown and stared into her eyes, "Are *you* okay?"

Luz smiled dumbly and said, "Uh-huh." The dude was hot, Luz thought. He was black with a close haircut. He also had a light mustache that matured his features and he had set of the best lips she'd ever seen. He licked them and extended his hand out to her, "I'm Theodore Nelson. But my friends call me Ted." Luz shook his hand and babbled, "M-My name is Luz Lopez. My friends call me Luz." Ted laughed at that and said, "Okay, Luz. You don't look like you're from here? I don't think I saw you around North Creston before."

Luz shook her head nervously and blushed, "Oh, u-um, I'm from New York. I just came to support my cousin for her special day."

He looked enlightened at her explanation and snapped his fingers. "Oh, you're Simone's cousin. Yeah, I heard about you."

Luz frowned. "Gee, I didn't know I was that notorious." Ted chuckled deeply and Luz had to remind herself that she had a boyfriend. She saw now that she needed to get herself back to Queens as fast as possible before she did something she shouldn't.

Ted sighed and said, "Well, who could forget the girl that lost her boyfriend to a coma and moved away to her loony cousin's house in New York. Yeah, word spreads fast around North Creston."

Luz felt offended that those people would take the pain from Simone's life and make it into Trenton's Hot Topic. "You know what; you people are a bunch of low lives." Disgusted, Luz turned around to storm off but Ted grabbed her arm and said, "Hey, hey, I'm sorry if I offended you. I really am."

Luz crossed her hands across her chest and pouted, "That was rude, yo." Ted came closer to her and licked his lips. He leaned down and said seductively, "Let me make it up to you. Dinner tonight at seven, I'm buying."

Luz rolled her eyes and said, "I'll be gone by seven. I'm going back to New York today. Sorry pal."

Ted made licking his lips a habit and Luz found it even more difficult to say no to him. Joey...she had to think of him...Joey. Looking around, Ted leaned in

221

and said to her, "Well, how about now? Let's ditch this place for some McDonald's or something. How 'bout it Luz..." Jeez, and the way he said her name was enough to make her tackle him right then and there. She swallowed and said petulantly, "W-Well, I can't just up and ditch Simone on her special day." Yeah, that was a sure way to make him go away. Ted scanned the place again and said pointedly, "Oh, really? It seems like Simone took her own little vacation." Luz looked around herself and saw that he was right. That's right; Seth had told her he had something surprised planned for her. Luz sighed and studied his sullied gown. "Well, I did stain your gown..."

Ted linked his arm through hers and they began toward the parking lot. Luz smiled and thought what Joey didn't know wouldn't hurt him. Besides, this was only innocent fun.

This was gonna make awesome gossip for Reina later on.

GEORGIA

It would be fair to say that Georgia hated Simone in the beginning.

After all, her evil ass father did throw her brother in jail after discovering he robbed that jewelry store. It wasn't his fault that he had a family to feed. They were so poor back then that even her parents were selling drugs to keep them financially afloat. Jerome was only being the best brother he could be, and that meant providing for his family—something Zachary Randon didn't seem to understand, because he failed them. When her father, Troy Cooper, scored the high paying retail job in Philly the family moved there for a while. Once Jerome got out of jail, he came back and convinced the family to move back to New Jersey. It was later on when he and Georgia devised a plan to get back at Mr. Randon for failing them and sending Jerome to jail in the first place. They decided to attack the most vulnerable person in the family: Simone Randon. She'd been an easy target at first because she was the trusting virgin and daddy's little girl that had secrets. She provided to be a simple way to procure the information to the Shay's case. It only took a little snooping around the Randon household to get it.

Yeah, Georgia was, in a lot of ways, wiser than her years.

Georgia had a change of heart when she realized that Simone wasn't that bad a person. Even though Seth had proved to be a major problem with her and Jerome's plans to ruin Simone, what happened to him would have probably been why Georgia decided to drop the grudge she had against her father. It was pointless, and Jerome was a brute that needed to be imprisoned anyway. And that was another thing that drew Georgia to her; her nicety. When Jerome came back from jail he'd been harder than ever, almost abusive, and Simone stood up to him for her. That was what tore it. Ever since then, she'd vowed to herself that she wouldn't harm the Randon's, because they'd been through enough. When Jerome put Seth in that coma she'd wished never succumbed to her brother's will that easy by getting revenge. And when he succeeded in causing that family pain, he succeeded in losing a sister, because at that point Georgia had lost all respect for him.

The graduation ceremony was coming to a close and Georgia sat back and finished her punch. The crowd was thinning and from the corner of her eye she saw Simone's cousin, Luz, ditching the party with her ex boyfriend and graduate, Teddy Nelson. Georgia shook her head and smiled deviously at what she had planned for the crazy whore.

After all, old habits died hard and, in Momo's words, she *really* wasn't that nice...

Hope You Enjoyed The Book!

Here's An Excerpt To *Edge*, The fourth Installment In The *Real* Series Written By My Sister, Laurie Ross

ENJOY!

EDGE

Kenna Chaplen lost her virginity to a clown.

I couldn't really think of any other name for myself at the moment. Though I guess that's what I get for getting drunk, raiding a costume shop, and sleeping with the enemy's sister.

What the hell, right?

Let's start over: I, Kale McAllen, am the "cool kid in town' with the heart of a servant and mind of a king. No, really. I could basically care less to the looks people would give me if they found out about me at this point. The clown.

Then why the hell was I here?

I turned to Kenna and tried to shrug off the drunken sleep pulling at me. She blushed and looked at my chest with a giggle. "You're a freak, you know that?" I said. I meant what I said. Who screws a clown? I rolled my eyes and fought the sickness of the vodka. Kenna frowned and whispered, "I know. I kinda have a thing for clowns. Don't know why; they're sexy to me. And you-"she reached for my mask but I smacked her hand away. Kenna chuckled softly. "- are sexy without the costume. Whoever you are Mr. Yummy. This body is a dream." She rubbed my tattooed torso and began to inch closer but the door burst open to reveal Corey. The enemy. And from the way he was glaring at me, an even angrier brother. I *had* to stop drinking.

ABOUT THE AUTHOR

Since the age of twelve, Laura could always be found writing. She writes within a wide array of genres, including paranormal, drama, slice of life, and (her favorite) romance. In her free time, if she's not writing, she's reading or listening to a steamy audio-book. Her most notable works include Something About Kyle and her ongoing, The REAL Series, which explores the narratives of various, interconnected young adults.

As an author, Laura aims to push boundaries and leave a lasting impact on her community. Her journey taught her the importance of perseverance, creativity, and staying true to one's unique vision. Support her craft by purchasing from her bookstore.